NACO PINK

CHRIS DIETZ

HNS Publishing | Bisbee, Arizona

NACO PINK

ISBN: 978-1-7335729-4-1

Cover Image: Chris Dietz
Book Design: Bill Dietz

HNS Publishing
Bisbee, Arizona

For Kaylen
(Please wait to read until your mom says it's ok)

Chapter One

I think every time I'm getting ready for a run out here, I think I slowly raise my head to pretend I've suddenly discovered there are mountains in my front yard, the surprising vision to the north. I think I pace my drama this way, because looking leads to unveiling where exactly we live. We live in the apron, the bare upheaval undulations that go around the mountains, not walling off the blast zone below, but girding the mountains to a sky island scald, above the blast zone, but it's *my* blast zone, and I think, I am the mountain right here. We live in the great in between, not the mountains, not the desert, uplifted on the down low. My right lace is shredding. I tie it up with a trick which includes a twist and a doubling. No biggie, these are my off road shoes for practice. I save my good shoes for meets. How embarrassing is that, to be one of the kids on the church's track team who has to use the team's spare pair. Donna Pardo has the other spare pair. I just like saying *spare pair.* But Mom and Dad work too much as it is, they couldn't get me any. I work too much. I tie my hair back, brunette spider threads. My stretches feel electric, I feel jumpy, my feet curl antsy, toes pressing together.

The Apache Mountains in my front yard used to be covered with green, trees, like piñon and juniper, but gray mountains still go up to the blue sky. Seems like a movement to me. Ascent! It's so clear I can see to heaven — I remember thinking at church when I was little. It's not cold either, couple t-shirts and a sweatshirt all I got on, so I won't be sweating like a pig. The mountains tumble up far as they can go, then they tumble down, down to this apron surrounding the mountains, so this in between like foothills before dead desert plain. We used to find weird stacks of white boulders around here, like stockpiles, like sculptures. Who built it? One time we discovered a hole with no bottom. We knew because we tested it, dropped in soda cans, rocks, bottles, then counted Albuquerques, but never heard an impact. That neverending hole is a pore for the tips of mountain roots, pushing through, exploring. The apron is in between scraggly mountains and what is politely called basin. Not much water in this basin. People are leaving: consolidate or die. For us, who stick around, home in the blast zone.

I flex my shoulders, push up my spine, hear it crinkle, neck extended. I wiggle my shoulders to center my little backpack. It's got my phone (turned off!) and a bottle of water. I jump in to a slow take off, assuming the form, watching my breathing, controlling it. I know what's ahead. I know every step of the way. I know every look. It's like with the mountains, when you know a thing close to you, your molecules get mixed up, your self and your place all mixed up. My molecules are turned on under my skin, deep in my cells. I feel it all the way down to my enzymes, zipping through my blood, hitting triggers, receptors, bonding, breaking bonds.

Dribble used to say, 'Know your molecules,' and we'd

all laugh, then he'd say, 'I was born with a microscope in my hand,' and the kids would groan and the females who'd had kids would go pfft with a 'no way, man.' Dribble's been our mentor for eons — maybe a year plus. He's proven to us that the overwhelming juggle of infinite infometrics has a way in. Back door, front door — sneak in...it don't matter. But IN you must git. When information is readily available on our phones, we got to have a way to work it, make it our own. Pick a topic! Civil War! Break it down! Sides, economics, tactics, slavery. Find the consistent point of view. Mexican War! Break it down! Sides, economics, indigenous voices. Who are the Mexicans? Where did they come from? Mestizos! Mixed blood. Never heard that. Never worried that. These words strut forth, juicy words, begging to be used. We discern, appraise, resolve. Dribble says we must decide its value. What matters. He's always blabbing, 'Do it yourself!'

This is my favorite run, each station contains multitudes — break it down! Scenes must be realized. Here comes Hot Dog, Chihuahua nightmare mix of ratty hair and pus nodules dotting his body, like he's got a case of bubble wrap skin. He pops over from the loquat tree under which he perches in the otherwise bare front yard next door. He jumps in place running beside me, two actions at once, but never touching me, barking all the time, serious mechanical yaps that a squirt of oil might fix. He vibrates, I swear he's a wind-up toy, but a fancy one that has all the apps. I don't even break my stride, I enhance my boundary vibe which he minds. Hot Dog's gear ratio simmers down. I tell him to go home. He doesn't last a block, then moving sideways, at an angle, tilted, like a crab (never saw a crab), he spirals around, back to his station under the loquat. Curve billed thrashers own that tree. They like to tease him, their big bird brains with clear orange eyes see right in to dog food brains, with that terrifying bird ESP, which is maybe why you don't see many thrashers any more. I think they're friendly. (Never saw a beet until I went over to Mona's.) The old lady who lives with Hot Dog is Ms. Cline. She and Hot Dog argue all the time. They have these random drag out brawls, so my dad, if he's home, will threaten to stick his head out the window and scream at them to shut up. Don't you know you can't argue with a dog! Or a woman, he'll want to add. If Mom's home, she'll threaten to knock his block off if he does. He never raises his voice.

Another block down Boras, past houses with people, families, then vacant houses that look superannuated. They're beyond haunted, they're obsessed with ghosts that sit on each other's shoulders now, conjuring entirely new entities. Right on his mark: here comes Spike! Bigger than Hot Dog, but brown, skinny, no pus, long legs like chopsticks, tail like a riding crop. Sad eyes. Another boy dog with his business cut off. Maybe some kind of terrier? Not sure what a terrier looks like. Ah, it's a whippet. Never seen one! Just a word from the vats of the info dumps. People like dogs in all shapes and sizes. So it's good, like Dribble says, that dogs' genetics are plastic (his word). A genetic pool — Gene Pool this dood I knew in 6th grade — easy for mutations to appear. Or is that a bone thrown to teenagers, that hints that we can mutate out of this? Like in a comic book? Nope. No relief in sight. People like real ugly dogs, Hot Dog and Spike both loathsome little mutants.

Spike doesn't last either. He sticks out his nose to sniff my sneakers, and that's as close as he comes. He heads home. He doesn't bark as much, and more of a moaning to his bark, like mournful, but not quite a howl. He's in despair. Last dog on Earth. Boras hits Cora, and Cora goes left or right, north or south. I go left, south. Quickly, pass the last house. Our hood was the first suburbia of Coltrane built away from Old Town. Now it's more than half empty, these three bedroom, two bathroom ranch style, sump block jobs, filled with mutant dogs (my parents won't have a dog — say we're too busy), ghosts, and cockroaches. Blank houses at the edge of the blast zone, like they belong here. Accoutrements. But they don't go on forever! A tiny farther little bit and I'll be free, and I'll do the creosote / mesquite zigzag on Mars, scrupulous enough to pretend it's interesting, open enough for a good trail. My feet get the pattern down. I can hear it. I can count the steps, but my watch is taking care of that for me. The view comes up — clear. The vast bowl of the valley to the west, cut by the river, I can see the way the land sweeps around — it curves, the *barrada*, which makes me excited to know it, and I feel it inside me like molecular gravity. The San Pedro River, and history is along the rivers, especially out here, this border country of overlap and misprision, and the river snakes a line right down the middle of the valley. The distant Huachucas, clear over on the other side of the barrada, are far more dramatic, and taller that our Apache Mountains.

Funny how routine works on a person, my stations, because I wait for the exact moment to take a look, my view of the view — the view goes on forever, but it doesn't, but it seems like that. That's not just eyes either. Seeing works in many ways. Dribble insists we use what we have, take advantage of what we know. We grumble, 'We don't know anything!' Dribble's using psychology on us, because it doesn't take a rocket scientist to know that *what we have* is *what we are*. Dribble points out access points to area history, how it was, what folks believed, in Pattern Recognition, our mentoring program through Testing. Lots of new words that only make sense as new words. He says use them in a sentence. Words are necessary to say it. I HAVE blast zone consciousness. I KNOW where to find the tracks across the lay of the land. And Dribble says the lay of the land was a way of the land. Changing Woman was all through here and way down in to Mexico, where they called her Tonantzin. She was the heart and womb of the land, its creative force. But it makes sense to see how Changing Woman would sit here, or stand here, or run here (those Indios ran too!), and know the importance of this view. To the south, distant foothills of the Sierra Madre in Mexico complete the view perfect. Palette of gray, brown, dirty yellow, and white-gold, dried up colors. Exhausted colors.

Dribble pushes Peggy, too. Which's a funny way to put it, blaming it on some poor girl who probably doesn't even know. Peggy, stands for P.E.G.F.I 'P' for population changes (not just overpopulation), the huge shifts in world population movements, due to 'E', environmental collapse, climate change, like running out of water, or too much water. Then the 'G', genetic manipulations plowing ahead without bothering about long term affects. All made worse with the return to 'F', fundamentalism. Meanwhile, 'I', for Information Technology, is hacked, manipulated, abused, until technology, finally — it's what happens in the books, is going to figure it can work a lot more efficiently without the interference, and distraction, of organic corpuscles.

Now I've gone over the sins of the world, so I can get to the next station. Here is where I get off the road, I know the exact spot, down a sandy slide by a culvert, and into Greenbrush Draw. It's an arroyo cut deep across the desert plain, from here to Naco about five miles due south, at the border. Now that illegals are hardly ever seen around here, and ever since the legalization of marijuana, Greenbrush Draw is pretty safe, and a sweet place to run, some slippery spots with sand or gravel. Usually, the draw is wide enough so it's easy jogging right down the middle. I descend to the draw. Descent! *Entrar arroyo.* The walls are over my head. I can't see over the walls. The tops, prickle thick with thorns, tangly to the edge, mesquite and creosote. Brush world! Lucky draw, the coolest place to run, right down the center, clear straight path. I'm not going all the way to the border, but I'll do 2-3 miles, then turn around. I've been coming here at least once a week since about a year ago, when I started track and needed a place to practice. Sometimes, some of the team comes over for a run with me. They like it, too. I like it alone, too. I let go and just run. Nothing to think about at all, cause I went over the official list. I be tracking. Boom.

Roots thick as my ankles slither down the arroyo's sides in snakes and squids of coiling drapes tacking up the wall sinuosity. Slabs of bark with lichen berries in cloudy greens and blues. I think that's what they are. Lichens in the desert? I think I saw a dump about fungal spores hitching a ride on dust particles in desert air. I breathe superfine, I guess, cause I'm used to it. Bushes and weeds in clumps. Grassy spots. I slow down, angling through a patch of small trees, sidestep, like willows, and those tobacco trees kids try to smoke in 8th grade. I sidle through, one-two-cha-cha-cha, slowing me down. It smells outside down here, heady mix pickle of chemically dust, spores, not too much garbage. Chunks of rusted metal, in heaps of iron butchery, then broken pipe with jagged, ragged ends that look like the heads of enraged eels. Plastic water bottles like cocoons. My eyes cocoon butterflies, break out, see off. Regain my pace, skirt a muddy spot. The walls are sandy, now, in places reddish as Mars. Pretty quiet. No bugs. No crickets. A few winter birds, the birds that stayed, our neighbors, our fellow travelers in the blast zone, but none around today. It's end of December, so I would guess life forms are hibernating dreams now. Do aminals leave ghosts? What with Peggy, no one cares. No one gives attention to that which is not given attention. Intent! Duh peeps are jonesing on survival alone now. In the great mean time, we gotz media meme traction machines. Distractions. Disruptions. We smother to death in the complete inventory of infinite imagery at our disposal. Whatever happens immediately links to its image from TV or movies. New Year's in a few days. Then back to work and study. Not now! Not now! No worries —

In this part of the draw cottonwoods have collapsed. I see it happen: a big wind comes up, or maybe the earth shakes, and the proud cottonwoods, dry as bones, crack and heave, cackling to the ground. No one around to see it or hear it, but me. Decaying logs flop on top of each other, so all sorts of hidey holes peeking out. Anyone home? I bet all kinds of rats live back there. Molecular rats with buckteeth and antenna. *Oh, Changing Woman, what have we done!* Who lives back there? Too teeny for pigs or coyotes. I've seen pigs out here once, and they were more scared of me. Broadside, pigs look huge, big as dogs. But head on, if you see them headfirst, like coming at you, they are thin as cardboard, and you wonder if they are cutouts. I have eyes, they go see what's in the hidey. I run on, but my eyes go on in, to a cuddly furry nest in a pocket of entwined limbs.

My breathing is even. I'm going too slow, taking it too easy. A straight stretch comes up. At its end, pretty far away, a white boulder sticking out of the side. Fix my eyes on it. Charge! Wind sprint speed! Feet up! Fists pumping. Full throttle. The white boulder makes a white surface, that my squinting eyes make a white sign, like a surprise billboard, with a long word printed on the sign with my name in it in the middle, MYA. Like that, all caps, in big letters. That word — I have to remember it! The whole thing!

Dribble says that arroyos are cracks in the desert, from the water table sinking. It's a different world from what it was. He says Changing Woman would not recognize her desert now. I tell Dribble, 'This is our home.' 'Me, too,' he goes. He's so funny as a mentor. But, yeah, I get what he means about how you have to find the pattern behind the dump. But, still, we'll all have to leave here. We know the end is near here, like any every day.

Run in the arroyo, crack in the world, this is my home. I can feel my body cooling after the sprint. Break a sweat. Up ahead, the draw makes a curve, so there's usually a ton of debris, rain or no, and today it's a massive clot of disgusting crap. No way I can get through it.

Dribble says there was a time when education meant a bunch of guys — girls weren't invited, sitting under the spreading chestnut tree thinking out loud. But what does that mean to us today, I ask Dribble. He goes, like every adult asshole ever, 'You have to figure that out for yourself.' He's been our teacher a long year.

Education is Testing. Everyone goes to the same school, like traditional face-to-face classes, through 6th grade, then you start Testing, go for training, internships, all the while online dumps to support your vocation. Most kids just use their phones. More Testing, special training, usually at the place you're going to end up working, far away. Or for those who Tested successfully to try for university, there is weekly, face-to-face mentoring. Pattern Recognition is what it's called.

I have to stop at the clot. It's that dense. There's bed

springs, balled up barbed wire, plastic water bottles, a toaster with its cord hanging down, like a rubberoid noose. Wonder what would happen if I plugged it in. If I tasted its crumbs, in the old bread slots, I'd know the last breakfast it hosted. I wish a gargantuan clawed arm would reach out and shove all this shit out of the way.

I figure the more I read, the more I'll be ready for my finals. Dribble's got me reading a lot of different things, not just dumps on a monitor. Books. But I also know it's pretty impossible: I have no money. I don't know anyone who has any money. I figure I'll join the Marines for four years, then use the GI Bill to go to university. So I study, I run, I read.

Jolt!

Heat flush rush from my spine outwards, to the tips of my fingers and toes!

Electric sizzle!

What?

— jump back with full body electrocution. My whole body hiccoughs. I could puke. I could pee. I freeze. I stare. Right in front of me, a big clawed arm pushes through the crap, draws it aside. Claws like tinker toys, thick and woody, attached to a shaggy hand bigger than my head.

Aminal! This aminal! Animal! I'm seeing, breathing, teetering!

It's over my head. Tall, tall, ginormous! And the clawed arm heaves back, finishing the job, clearing the junk from the bend in the draw.

I don't know what I'm looking at. I know it's in front of me. Monster Bear! Hundred feet tall! Thick! Thick brown fur, heavy limbs. Massive! Slow moving. Bottom half shaggy with legs thick as stumps. He stands there, hairy melon head, eyes like a cow's, surveying the scene, now that he's done the deed. Head like a hairy turtle. No! His head comes back around so his eyes find my eyes, and I make sure — yup, he's a he. I shrug. He shrugs, then a shake of his head. But like in slow motion. Time differential. I see, I see, I see. That head is not like a bear's at all. Kind of doofus looking. I don't know why I'm not running back the way I came, screeching my head off. Big dood did me a solid.

Maybe I'm hyperventilating. Ms. Winter, our track coach, says to watch for that. My breathing is superfine. He's just standing there, like hovering, like he's waiting. I don't even know if he likes me. From the corner of my eye, movement! Down the arroyo wall, knights attack! Knights in armor jump, fall, tumble in. But strangely silent. No clack, clack, clack of armor static. Shiny! Shiny, silver armor! Knights! They wear those weird pinched helmets. Not a single scream or holler. They wield long spears with evil metal tips. They attack the bear. I press down, squeeze down as hard as I can —

I'm running down the draw and I glance at my watch. Two and half miles. Far enough. I think I took it too easy. I can make up for it on the way back. I come to a stop in a wide area. I'm on the west side, hunkered down. Breathing, breathing, breathing. I stretch a sec. I jiggle my pack around to get out my water bottle to have a drink. Not too much. Return it, push my pack back in place.

I hear a car engine. I smell exhaust. No, it's too loud. It's a truck. Now, I see it. A dirty, green and black truck backs in to the other side of the draw, the east side. If it backs any more the tires are going over —

A crazy banging up front of the truck, what's gotta be someone's openhanded slaps across the truck's body, on the passenger side, then a guy appears, rushing back to check it out.

"Dood," he calls, "too close, too close! Move, move up! Few feet."

The truck jerks forward. The guy clambers back, holding on to the truck. He calls, "That's good. *Bueno.* Stop! Stop!"

The truck goes into idle. It turns off. The other door up front bangs open. Another guy, an almond-shaped man with a pointed pink head, must be the driver, saunters over all giddy like, like he's striking a pose. He examines how close he came. He glances at the other guy. "Perfect. Right at the edge. I told you I could do it with my eyes closed. Just feel it out."

"Great, man."

"You wanna do the honors?"

The other guy grabs hold of the side of the truck and swings up on the little lip around the back. He messes around with the central gizmo. Unlocks it. Or unhooks it. He rolls up the back like a garage door. He steps on in, messes with the controls some more, unfolds the lift from where it gets tucked away. Big black barrels back in there with him.

The guy on the outside goes, "There's a lot of them."

The guy inside the truck says, "Two at a time, on the lift."

"Yessir, jefe!" He belches gross.

The guy in the truck moves to a barrel, bends over as though to hug it, clasps it, tilts it up on its side. He straightens, rolls the barrel forward to the edge. It happens fast, as though he were doing sleight-of-hand, like he's a juggler, and any sec he could lose control. The barrel is positioned on the lift. He goes for the next barrel. He shushes out a, "This is the hard part."

"Ah, amigo. Burp. Burping. We take turns. Burp. It's my truck. I own the truck."

"Bank owns the truck." He rolls the second barrel forward, gets it in place.

"I make the deals. Hector, don't. This way — "

"What way? Hit it, Ted."

Ted pushes the button and the barrels get lowered. Now Ted has to wrestle them off the lift to the sides. He's not as smooth about it as Hector. He makes the lift go back up. He pulls a big wrench from his back pocket. Must have stuck it back there when I couldn't see him get out of the cab. He fiddles with some big nuts on top of the barrel right in the center. He wrenches at it. The top comes off. He takes to the side of the barrel, hands grasping the top edge, and leans it forward over Greenbrush Draw.

"Easy, easy," goes Hector. "Gotta save the barrels. They're worth something."

Finally, a critical angle is reached, and this fat mucusy glug percussions across the draw, as a tidal wave of thick pink goo belches out of the barrel to pour in a gusher down the side of the draw, then into the draw, covering plants, sticks, logs, metal bits, quickly beginning to form a pond. It doesn't take long and Ted pulls up the barrel and rolls it to the side. By now, Hector has another two loaded, so Ted brings them down, rolls them off, raises the lift. He gets back to work with the big wrench. He opens each barrel at the top, then leans it over the edge to vomit pink goo.

It goes on and on like an assault. Expelling of the pink. Expulsion! Expectoration. Exudation. Splashing, dripping... Earth glops pink. Disgusting. I want to run. I can't stop spying. The wound maker brings his own blood. Thick, sweet smelling sludge rivers in pink rivulets, pink puddling to a pink lake of pink.

Poison!

"Bismuth," says Hector.

Ted stops what he's doing with the wrench, puts his arms out and up, hands flailing. "Okay, we take a loss here. Who knew they wanted the stuff bottled? For the price, it was worth it. We took a chance."

"No one else interested?"

"Our guy controls all the dollar stores on the border. Only show in town, man. They're like dealers, pimps, man. Poor people's addiction to junk food? Tell me about it! Come on, let's get this done."

"Mr. Dollar." He snorts, breathes, pants. "Do you want to switch? I'll dump. You put 'em on the lift?"

"Sure, but first let's get these empties back on the truck. We're getting there."

"I'll have to do some rearranging. Push these to the side."

"How many more?"

"Five."

They get busy, and I take off, bending low, making a smaller target. Glad I wore my old gray sweatshirt, and not my new turquoise one. Fast now, I plow down the draw. No! I won't turn back for a last, enzymatic look, as though to make sure it happened. My eyes are playing me today. Making my body see, too. All eyes. I'll keep running, watch my form, watch my feet, keep the breathing even. A fluttery sound from a cluster muster of weeds. Feathery sound? See it!. Sounds familiar, sounds soothing. Quail? Quail soothing to me? There are a few left. People don't eat them anymore, because of the virus or the bacteria or the metals. I can't remember which. They don't leave for Christmas. Now, boom, my clot! Still miraculously unclotted. I don't even slow down to check it out, don't look for helmets or toasters or giant bears. I am focused on my running, my breath. Not a worry in my head.

Worry won't start until later.

When I get home, nice and winded, the good burn, Dad's home. He's in the living room in front of the TV watching the news and drinking a beer. He looks like a statue of a dad like that...so worn and tired and stiff. His eyes are puffy. He works for the county, has to cover a lot of jobs they used to have a lot of men do. What would be the point of complaining. His family's been around Coltrane for four generations. His grandpa worked underground.

"I'm home," I say.

He gets up slowly, trudges over to me in the kitchen with a sweet smile across his face. He's one of those guys with a big face, as though his head were extra large. Maybe it's just because his eyes are so puffy, his face looks puffy. He gives me a hug. He loves driving around the desert, four wheeling. He loves the mountains, the valley, even the desert We used to go hiking in the mountains. "Good run," he says softly. I can hear the exhaustion in his voice.

"Good run," I say.

He goes back to sit in the living room.

I query, "World falling apart?"

"Worse every day. We still got those beans and homemade tortillas?"

I nod, though I know he can't see me, but it's part of our routine, what we go through night after night, especially when Mom's not home. "Mom working late?"

"Double shift."

"I'll fix us something."

I go to the bathroom to pee and wash up. Water's clear, but I avoid getting it in my mouth. I come back out and head for the fridge. I take out the bowl of refried beans, the tortillas Mom got from someone at work, and some green chile salsa I made. I get the beans in the microwave, then put the fry pan on the good burner, get the gas going, double check it. I get out plates and forks, set the table for two. The microwave dings. I put tortillas in the hot fry pan.

"Come and eat."

Dad whoops, comes over to join me at the table with his beer.

After we eat and clean up, Dad doing the dishes,

while I put stuff away, I go back to my room to see what's up. I turn on my phone, start checking things. The phone is expensive so I have to watch how I use it. I pay for it every month with my own money.

Texts from Mona. An email from Dribble about our session tomorrow. Some kids on the track team want to get together for a run. Testing doesn't have teams any more. No money, so no extra-curricular activities. No sports. No clubs. So in the last couple years, churches from all over started sponsoring intramural teams for kids. All ages. Keep 'em busy. Even if you don't go to that church, it's something to do together.

Mona phones. "What you up to?"

"'Bout five foot nine."

"That never gets old."

"What you?"

"You know this you, my you sitting in Naco house watching parental units meditate."

"You do that a lot."

"Hey, hippy parents, man, like watching grass grow. You know how guys like to watch concrete set? Watch it get all stiff and hard?"

"You're watching your parents get stiff?"

"Guys like road work."

"I like road work."

"Yeah, means somebody got a job. You went running."

"Besides, that's sexist. Some boys don't like road work. If you were brought up with a bunch of boys always playing with trucks, building cities in the mud, you'd like road work too."

"That's incongruous. How would you know, anyway, you don't have any brothers."

"Either do you."

"Single daughters. It's like a thing. Maybe hippy parents just have daughters?"

"It's a coincidence. My parents weren't hippies."

Mona hangs up.

That was fruitful. I don't want to study. I don't want to read. I don't want to watch TV. I think of Ted and Hector, and their cargo. Should I call someone? Report it? Who would pay? You call the cops or the sheriff now, you get charged. What if I imagined it? No way. I didn't. I know I didn't. I know the diff.

I have this book. Dribble's. I look up the dood. It's like an overview to here, but from 10,000 years ago. Great picts. Lithics. Bone tools. Ah, Megatherium. Giant ground sloth. Yes. Thought I recognized him. My buddy. Did the Conquistadors encounter them?

I get out a notebook, a pen. I turn to the back of the notebook to the blank pages. I write, AYADEMYAVICHY. I can't tell if that's it exactly. I try to visualize the word on the white billboard boulder. I think that's it.

If I tell Mona, she'll get distracted. She gets distracted too easily. She can't afford that right now. It's tough. Her parents get some kind of pension, but it's not much. They live off less than we do. Beans and rice, that's it. They have this tiny place in Naco. If they didn't meditate so much, it would be worse, everyone bumping into each other all the time. Mona has to stay focused. She's in Pattern Recognition with me. We met in Testing when we were twelve. She professed to speak Latin and Greek back then. She'd go off on these adorable, little girl speaking in tongue routines. I wasn't taken in by her pretend, I was incredulous at what a great liar she was. We been friends ever since.

Actually, the truth is simpler, more pathetic. My name, Mya, is often mispronounced around here, and it has been since I was little. Most people, even relatives, pronounce it Me-Ya. Mona knew right away it was My-a.

Kids don't know each other like they used to. We were lucky. You see kids hanging out in movies or TV from back in the day, and they're all so into how they look, who they're sleeping with. Now, there's no student body. There's no place to hang out, except, of course, every American teenager's secret beer bash lair, off a dirt road in the blast zone. Different training, different Testing, make work, employment the priority, the number one focus to get out of here. I'm lucky to have my shitty job. It's only fifteen hours a week but that's more than most kids. The county has me come in three times a week to scrub their facilities. Kids around here, now, they wouldn't stick to Coltrane or Naco if their parents didn't have something going on. The last hustle before it all dries up. Now, I am just plain stupid, demented cemented, depressed, heartbroken, resentful, bitter.

The phone rings. It's Mona.

I say first, "You hang up on me?"

"Listen, amoeba, freak out news coming in from Naco— "

"Chupacabra?"

"Listen! I got a text that this old lady who lives out by the old fort saw a pink skunk in her yard."

"Pink?"

"Listen! Then the same girl who texted me, who heard about the skunk from her *tia*, who knows the old lady, sent another text. Her *tia* just saw a pink roadrunner in her yard."

Chapter Two

Hector says, "What day is it?

I go, "Tuesday or Thursday." My breakfast burrito has crawled through my guts all day, like a slug of lard, and now it's hung up in the groinal area like an acrobat banana. I'm gonna have to hold it.

"It's Monday," he explains, in that voice, with that tone like he's talking down at me.

"All right! Monday all day long." I burp.

Hector rolls his window down. No wind, not too cold. He sticks out his head, pulls it in. "No difference no more between weekdays and weekends. Don't even think about Christmas."

"Ah, you didn't get any presents. No holidays."

"Remember cards? My ma always sending cards to my grandma. Something she did."

"Birthday cards! Yeah. Hallmark's MIA, dood. We got

TV and dollar stores. And prisons. All that's left. Ain't anything like we thought it would be."

"No zombies. You know where this place is? The turn off?"

"For sure. We dump it, take the barrels back, hose 'em down. We're good."

I downshift, burp, the truck shudders. My eyes are peeled for the turn off. Both sides of Naco Highway are pure brush going on forever. Invisible landmarks. I'll see it. I'll see it first. Hector wants more. A joke? A fart. What were we talking about? Tuesday or Thursday? Haven't slept. I don't sleep. Then the dreams. I got nobody hunting for me, wanting to kill me. Simple joys. No complaints. Under the radar. If there *were* zombies, at least, you'd know what your enemies looked like. There's nothing. Nothing's a vacuum. Couple more loads and I get caught up. We're working here.

I say, "It doesn't feel like a Thursday."

Hector grunts, "Every day's Thursday now, day before pay day, day before Friday, day before something's gonna happen."

Now what's he talking? I gotta find that road. It's just dirt. Bare scratch through the filth, the mummified bitch goddess of the desert. My partner, the philosopher. Everybody's a philosopher. 'Cept me. My folks neither. They moved to Coltrane in the 80s. They knew nothing about the mines closing. They were hippies and smoked pot constantly, which is how come I only smoke occasional: it's boring. Who wants to be like loser hippy parents? Ma got a job with the power company. Dad was sorta a mechanic. In Coltrane if you were not retired, an artist, or a Mexican, what you had to do was a little of this, a little of that. But they were never too good at one thing. Ma went up to Tucson with her agate collection when consolidation started. Dad disappeared. I didn't like Tucson. I like stray body parts of broken superheroes: all the action figures that bit the dust, now weird decorations, in pieces, across the blast zone, on the shoulders of every highway, easy to pick up, easy to clean up, easy to rebuild.

Hector goes, "No traffic. Nobody around."

"No nothing."

Hector snorts. "No one the wiser, no one cares. Illegal don't mean like it used to."

"We're not getting in any trouble dumping this load, Mr. Philosophy. It's all on the up and up. We got it going on! We take care of this, then back to Mexico to pick up a load. Papers are all in order. Churros, jefe! Bring the load across, over to the dollar store guy."

"Boring. When the cartels raged, you knew which side you were on."

"Yeah, shit your pants scared side! Oh, brother, don't make me puke."

"I looked it up. This stuff. It's bismuth."

"What the fuck is bismuth?"

"It's like an element."

"Your phone is crazy!"

The turnoff should be right here. It's gotta be right here! Now would be perfect. Now would work fine. In case I have to make an emergency pit stop. And there it is! Good thing I am sharp on it. I take it slow, swing the truck on to the dirt scrape.

"Here we go," I say. I take it careful, grip the steering wheel.

Hector comes back with, "The dollar store guy said he was interested. You said."

I don't like this way. Him always bitchin'...I could puke —

"He *was* interested. He needed it bottled. You wanna bottle it? We dump it, we're done. Man, it's bidness. It didn't work out."

"The profit from the chip delivery paid for it. I saw the dollar guy give you the check. We hit the bank. We went right back to Mexico for this shit."

"It was so cheap. He said he was interested."

"But you didn't tell him it wasn't bottled."

"You was there. Through the whole thing. You heard it too. We picked up the chips and the Mexican guy says he has ten barrels of this stuff. It was so cheap! We delivered the chips and asked the dollar store guy, sure he's interested. I'm the one taking the hit."

"Those were the worst chips ever."

"'scuse me, Mr. Gourmet Hog, we're doing a service here. Yeah, chips made out of sawdust, who the fuck knows, who the fuck cares."

"Dollar stores are all that's left."

"We got a gas station."

"True. A bank. City offices."

"County."

"What if you need a pair of socks?"

"Yeah — what?"

"Gotta go up to Tucson for a pair of socks."

"Consolidation, man."

"Dollar stores stink like meth labs used to. Tiny Naco has two dollar stores. Coltrane's gotta have four by now. Don't know how many in Douglas."

"Hector, that way is...that way's always trying to compare, trying to figure it. Burp. Then what? You're gonna feel better about things? Bullshit! Hector, how long you been with me?"

"Year."

"Steady wages?"

"Sure."

"Man, that's it, that's what's real. It was the luckiest day ever, you and me, teaming up this year. I cultivated my connections. We got a steady thing. Perfectly legal."

"Never thought I'd end up a chip mule."

"Yeah, well, I was not cut out for hauling illegal stuff. No way. No guns. No frigging contraband. No way. People all a sudden get mighty interested in you when you're moving shit. Then, geez Louise, they're looking for you, hunting for you. Out here in the blast zone. Hell with that! No way. Like living on borrowed time."

"That's for adrenaline junkies."

"Tweakers." The truck goes through a shallow spot. I slow it down. He's hanging out of the window.

He goes, "You gotta take it real slow here." He's quiet. Philosophizing, I guess. "It's so empty."

"Everybody's leaving."

"No work."

"We got it made, jefe!"

"Nada." He comes back in. "The occasional truck load of weapons going into Mexico apprehended, and it's big news. For about one second."

"We're set, man! We don't need no trouble."

"You and Mr. Dollar, regular bro's."

"Hey, I like that. Mr. Dollar. There's the draw. Check it out! Let's see here."

"Take it slow."

"Thanks for the advice. You always gotta give the advice."

"I can drive."

"Yeah, sure. Man, Mr. Dollar used to have me hauling stuff in from all over the west. Now, me and you, we got a set up. Mr. Dollar, our Mexican guy, all we gotta do is go over the line, pick up our load, take it back to Mr. Dollar."

"What would be the point of smuggling now — I mean, besides guns."

"I gotta turn around. Back in."

"When everyone's poor, living in a ghost town, the law's whatever you bother with. I slow to a stop. "I can turn in here." I start up, roll in to the weeds and crap. Hector leans out of the window again. He calls, "You should be okay now."

I hold it a second. "Mr. Philosophy, talking about how it was. Duh good ol' days.

Come on! Was it different before? You and me, people who've grown up 'round here, it's all we've ever known, the hustle. Think back to how it was when everybody had a gun. We'd be dead by now. That's for sure."

"Probably."

"We're okay. Mexican guy said he had churros. For next time. So yeah. Packaged. Good to go. Easy load. We dump this. Get rid of the barrels. We go back for the churros."

He says all hoity-toity, "I remember some book I read about World War II, and how this supply guy had a bunch of cheap chocolate sauce and a bunch of cotton balls, so he figured why the hell not, chocolate covered cotton balls."

"You read too much."

He shrugs, mumbles. He quits his skittish looking around, out all the windows. He squeezes out, "It's clear. Back on in."

"Easy as pie. Watch this. I line it up. I'll do it with my eyes closed."

Chapter Three

I'm standing at the side wall of windows in the old high school's library, facing the pseudo-quad. I'm a little early, I'm a little tea pot. Everybody's not here yet. It's here we meet for Pattern Recognition. Cecil gave me a ride in his mom's car, because she had to stay home with his sick little sister, and miss work at the bank where she's a teller. They don't really need tellers anymore, as most banking is done electronically, but his mom turned out to be really good with computers, a born hacker, even though she never went to college. Cecil's not in Pattern Recognition. I think he's done with Testing, lives down the street with his mom and sister, was going by anyway, on account of some guys he's meeting are trying to learn how to milk scorpions for big bucks in the venom trade. Dumps on everything. Except what to do when you've seen something ghastly. Pink world! Except out the window, sky blue comes down like an ocean. At eye level, buildings and people, faces between buildings, faces and walls, faces and hoodies, floaty faces. Robin's egg blue sky. What is robin's egg blue? I think real, real pale blue but not whitey. Robin's a bird. Never seen one. Plus,

Batman's sidekick. No one cares about pink. Pinky, the happy color. True blue attracts distraction, gentle on the eyes, foisting attachments, so I go for the opposite, push indoors, push official, push public. I'm cool, acting adult, in control, 'I'm a responsible — 'fill in the blank. I'm taking charge. (Notes for Mona! Always accumulating.) And it's a static charge. Blue blue charges land sinew. I'm like a battery. Recharging. Still, more in the Apaches here, mountains surround us, mountain backdrops connive each look. Ton of kids for all sorts of programs, extra training, but not nearly as many as it was. Blue goes to grayishness when it hits kids that look like shades. No playing around! Goofy, big mouth kids are distractions. Nobody in our group goofs or doesn't show. Blue. Mountains. Faces. Gray. Out the window, a cute guy my age walks straight towards me. I don't know him. I don't recognize him. My head hasn't moved. My eyes in his face aimed at mine. His eyes squint in the glare. He's looking at me. Walking straight towards me. And me. His eyes peer right in. He smiles. He's so cute. We could have a world together, float in the blue, hold each other still, while the Earth kept moving, in and out, side to side. He walks right on past. He was looking at someone else, that I couldn't see. He never opened his eyes to me. I don't think you can see in to the library. Glare goes *in*, but doesn't come out. Maybe it's my hair like this —

I choose life and decide to move away. The first thing you learn in gaming is keep moving. You hold still, you're an easy target. How Dribble managed to squeeze us in today nobody knows. We could use the extra time. This is the culmination of our program before Testing in the spring. But, today, what we got is Pattern Recognition, Tuesday after Christmas, in a dilapidated high school without water. But some heat, occasional heat. There's classrooms for Testing and training. A trailer has a free clinic. Our multi-purpose, old library serves fine. A couple outhouses and a port-o-pottie are open. I can see outhouses from here, beyond the high school, in among houses. They dot the town, now, poopy punctuation marks in the blank suburbs.

The library right this second is quiet, peaceful, safe. No pink. No intrusions. Our group has gathered at the back, at the table where we usually sit. They're all here. No sign of Dribble. A few book shelves remain, several rows of books. Around what would have been the central librarian desks, lots of defunct dictionaries and tattered encyclopedias. Ancient magazines are stuffed in shelves, then on the floor, pillars of them. Kids use them for collages. We all like to cut up stuff. Scissoring can be fun. At the other tables, littles, small ones, in groups doing work, students and adults. Mona's looking at magazines. I see her lips, her eyebrows. She has a stack beside her, at her spot at the table. There's only six of us, away from jobs and responsibilities, three guys and three girls.

Mona calls out to me approaching, "You're all sus." Not an accusation, but a sympathy note.

Hillary, who is sitting next to her, still with her hat on, croons, "'By the pricking of my thumbs —'"

Quentin finishes, "'— something wicked this way comes.'"

I go, "I said hey to you, Hillary. When I came in —"

Maybe no time off means no time to make friends. Every second sequestered to survival. Duty. Because that's all you can do. A lot of extra work not to be lonely. There's just no time.

Maybe pink means no pink off to make pink. Every pink sequestered to pink. Pink. Because that's all you can pink. A lot of extra pink not to be pink. There's just no pink.

Hillary goes, "Then you had to go look out the window, before I could say back — "

Quentin jumps in: "You hear about the Painter?"

Hillary adjusts her hat.

Mona says, "I told her last night. Cartoon characters coming to life in Naco!"

Somewhere, an adult shushes her.

Shepherd looks up from his big ass calculator he's working on to enunciate to all: "Right out of a game. We knew this would eventually happen. Crossover. Mash ups. Gigalips." He's wearing a new shirt, button down, pink. I can tell because it's so crisp, right out of its wrapper. Pink.

I protest, "What's a Painter?"

But Mona tsks at him: "You're a gore, dood. Gaming whore! Everything's in bits and bytes for you." Mona pushes aside her magazine, flips it closed, puts it on the top of the stack next to her.

"I'm writing code!" says Shepherd. He returns to his work.

Mona says, "And we're all so proud." She pauses dramatically, then she whispers her voice: "What if it's poison? Stench rot percolating up from the bowels of Changing Woman, to cleanse this hellhole. Or demons — demons run amuck. There's got to be a tear, a break, a bifurcation, in the space-time continuum, and it's leaking out demons who paint animals pink."

Quentin interrupts, "No pink coyote yet. You know what I think? The last graffiti border artist gone boots voltage. Think of it: living graffiti. Some old artist dood from Coltrane."

Mona nods appreciatively, exaggeratedly. "A last act of defiance? Coltrane artists are too old for chasing down road runners. Beep beep. No, I say it's a crack in the continuum, and horrific hog creatures, with ghostly ghastly fangs and talons, are sneaking out and vomiting up pink gore."

I've sat down opposite Hillary and Mona. I drop my pack in front of me. Mona catches my eye, says, "Your buddy's here." She raises her chin to point. She has a great chin, and she's drawn a black beauty mark on it today. I turn around. Donna Pardo.

"Hi? We doing the practice run out by your place. On Thursday. Right? Ten AM?"

"Sure," I smile.

"You heard about the Painter?" Donna smiles. She looks pink with a pink top and a pink smile.

"Oh, yeah," I say, "I know all about it. You Testing?"

"No, training. I didn't do too well on the tests."

"You'll do fine."

She smiles some more, turns and leaves.

I ask, "What's a Painter?"

Quentin mimics a philosopher from TV: "Pink crazy border artist, living graffito, getting us ready for New Year's."

"The Painter!" clarifies Hillary. "Sounds scary. You got Candyman, clowns from outer space, killer tomatoes, Freddy, Jason, Michael. And the Painter."

Quentin whoops, "We've seen the same movies!"

An adult intervenes: a warning...

Hillary frowns. She takes off her hat, a knitted job her mom made, the type stoners used to wear, like Grateful Dead kids my mom told me, and now she wads it up in her hands, then wraps her left hand in it.

Tremayne, who rarely talks but when he does we listen, who has watched everyone else talk now, his funny square head jerking to shift up his glasses, suddenly becomes a speaker: "What is the pink stuff? Mona's right. It could be anything — dangerous. Anyone tested it? It's not paint."

Quentin says, "How do you know?"

Tremayne says, "It would kill an animal to be submerged in paint."

Quentin says, "Alien goo."

Mona says, "It doesn't feel like a Wednesday."

Tremayne says, "BTW — I got your reference to WHH, but I'm not condoning your metaphor madness."

Hillary confesses, "I been binge watching *Melrose Place* on my phone."

Shepherd snaps to attention. "My mom likes that."

"But you don't," says Quentin.

Mona squeals. "Pareidolia, funny boy. Pareidolia,

all the way. Google it. It's what I suffer from, and you should show some empathy."

Tremayne says, "Who knows what form mutations will take? But, by definition, they'd be Earth critters mutating. From Earth, right? Not alien. Or extraterrestrial. Certainly not supernatural."

Hillary smirks at him in a flirty way. "You're all lit talking about this. The Painter."

Tremayne blushes. "It's a mystery."

Quentin cries, "It's a Christmas miracle!"

Mona huskily whispers, "I have a sighting."

Everyone turns to see Mr. Drabble hustling in. They quiet. The boys all release a sigh of relief in synchrony.

Shepherd starts sucking out ketchup packets he's brought out from his pack. Mr. Drabble says a lot of people do ketchup packets. You get a handful for a bean at the dollar store. He says their bodies tell them they need it.

Mr. Drabble wears his corduroy sports jacket with the elbow patches, over an old turtle neck sweater with holes in it. I can see the holes. He's wearing sandals. He always wears sandals. And with socks, of course. He has a big head, too, like my dad, but his isn't puffy with exhaustion, his is jowly with angst. He's got a sick kid. His wife's gotta stay home and care give. He hustles gigs all over the county. Now he's assumed his position at the top of our table. Every eye on him. He rolls his pack over his roly poly shoulders and dumps it in front of him. He's supposed to be the same species as us. He's looking us over.

He goes, "Happy Festivus!" But in a controlled voice, that is neither too loud or too quiet, the perfect decibel level.

Quentin blurts out, "Jackie Gleason!"

Hillary says, "Johnny Carson."

Tremayne giggles and we look at him. He's drumming the fingers of both hands in front of himself on the desk. They look like pink spiders, pink spiders.

"What?" says Mr. Drabble.

"Seinfeld," answers Tremayne.

Mr. Drabble claps, hoots, but quietly, carefully. "Give the man a prize. Boys and girls, this is Pattern Recognition. You've studied, you've read, you have the fundamentals, and now a new year approaches, so it would make sense to put those fundamentals to work, see what you can come up with. We consider what to *do* with information. We have been studying how to organize a response or exposition, starting with a setup or intro for background, then position statements, conjuring a proof. Analysis! Analyze. Break it down. Right? Use an outline! Outlines can really simplify organization. That's what we been doing.

"Okay, okay. We've seen there are different types of knowing. For example, the sciences and the Humanities. Each has its own methods, its own expectations. Outcomes. Now we play with it, experiment with it. Master it! We have confidence, because we know how to analyze. When the time comes, 'when the hurly burly's done,' you'll be able to deal with whatever they throw at you, verbal question or written test.

"I thought we'd do things a little differently today. Have some fun. Put down your pens. Lower your defiance shields. We'll start with me asking a couple questions, then you guys ask some questions. From there, we'll see what we get into. You know your assignment, your big paper's coming up. You know Testing's schedule, you know what you should be doing."

"Clear, boss," says Mona.

He clamors: "First question! Eyes straight ahead, on me. Don't look! How many people in our group are left handed? Don't guess. There's seven of us. Simple math. Don't answer now. Watch. Observe. We'll return to this later. Second question: how many people in our group have brown eyes? No guessing! Observation. Good! We'll answer these in a little."

I can tell Mona wants to yell out something nasty but she restrains herself. The others are jittery trying *not* to glance around at each other's hands or eyes.

Now, it's our turn:

I ask, "What's a lode?"

Hillary says, "You know about the Painter?"

Then a series of fast questions lashes out: "What's an arroyo?" "Where did the people east of Eden come from?" "If people your age are Millennials, what do you call people our age?" "Could the pink stuff be poison?" "I didn't finish the reading."

Mr. Drabble comes back with: "Occam's Razor: hoaxes, hysteria, subsidence."

An inhalation of breath sweeps across the table as though he has uttered sacred words.

I say, "Are we still asking questions?"

Mona says, "Razors ripped my flesh?"

"Sure," says Mr. Drabble, and I realize he's exhausted, too, and doesn't really know what to do today with us.

I ask, "What's a ley?"

Everyone laughs. Mona says, "Should I explain it to her?"

I go on, "How comes there was so much copper around here? How did it get so concentrated here?"

Mona raises her voice: "Girl's on fire! At the speed of thought!'"

Mr. Drabble says, "She's curious!"

Tremayne says, "The pink goo could be a slime mold."

Mr. Drabble hacks out a coughing laugh, goes for his water bottle in his pack. Books tumble out of his pack, textbooks and paperbacks, then discs, thumb drives. He takes a deep drink. We wait, watching his every tic obsessively. Adults! They are so fucked up. He comes up for air, begins:

"Arroyo is draw. Ditch. You know that. Lode's an ore body — see gold. Deep forces in the molten center of the Earth percolate up different metals depending on their density — see atomic weight. The interesting question is where do the metals come from, anyway? Not the Earth. Everything's made in the sun, the atomic cauldron. East of Eden is a mystery. Sometimes you just have to accept it. That's faith. Ley lines are imaginary electromagnetic lines over the Earth, that are supposed to roughly correlate to deep underground and/or ethereal forces. My generation were called Millennials, since we were born around 2000. You guys are being called Lassies. But I know you don't like that. We didn't like Millennials either."

Shepherd grumbles, "The last generation."

Mona quips, "Yeah, dood, hit the reset button."

"I didn't expect you to finish all the reading," says Mr. Drabble.

Hillary says, "Why did they write like that? Too many words."

Mr. Dabble asks, "The Montaigne or the Galileo?"

Hillary says, "Francis Bacon."

Quentin says, "He invented — wait for it! Tremayne, it's up to you?"

Tremayne says, "The scientific method."

"I was thinking bacon," says Quentin.

I go, "We got it, Mr. Drabble. The information you want us to be familiar with is duh stuff, then on top of this stuff we have to develop our own system of analysis. You want us to do a Midrash on the Enlightenment, like commentaries, annotations, finding the patterns. Four hundred years later, what do we know. The Enlightenment established our methods of analysis, right? How to do science, how to do law, how to do capitalism. Those guys, like Galileo and BLT, were there at the beginning, getting it started. Now, hundreds of years later and we gotta ask, did it work? Did it do any good? Was it worth it? We got to conduct an analysis of the doods who invented analysis." (I worked in the word analysis here, as that is his favorite word.)

Mr. Drabble nods his head but looks wary. He says slowly, "I'm on trial? We're on trial?"

Shepherd says, "I like that, Mya. You get cerebral angry, total geek out. Anyway — " he shrugs with enthusiasm, "science works."

Mona says, "Science is tools. Sure, they work. The Enlightenment, the scientific method, the sciences, they work. But slaves, man? It's all on the backs of other people. Tools we can use to figure stuff out. Groovy. To predict what's coming. Smart. But aren't we missing something? What was excluded? Who was excluded who would've helped? How come science is so tangled up with bondage, and I don't mean the fun kind?"

Mr. Drabble goes, "Show offs! Rabble rousers! Midrash? Did you really say Midrash? You guys talk around the five hundred pound gorilla in the room. No, I don't mean moi. Analyze! What is the context? Today — what is the context? After. The grand after. The after picture of civilization. Don't just criticize. Define your necessity. Have you defined your outcomes? What do you have to replace it? At least, to mitigate circumstances? I thought we were working on that? If you're not going to do it, who is? You know, in your spare time, save the world. So, thesis, antithesis, synthesis. Whichever way you argue, which ever method you use, make sure you feed the gorilla."

Now I feel (bored) we aren't getting anywhere today.

I mumble, "After, eh? We're at the end. They were at the beginning. The party's over. Big mistake. Your generation, the one before it, on and on, nobody could stop the snowball rolling into the blast furnace. Now, we gotta come up with something better. It's up to us now. That's what you want us to say."

Hillary says, "Too sad."

Mr. Drabble says, "Depends. But sure. Why not? Analysis grows from a perspective. New perspectives required. Like your point of view — POV. You know the issues. You know how we got here. But let's get back. The practical POV. What do you think is going to be on the test? Not just multiple choice — what's a plebiscite, type of dealio? They'll want comparisons, summaries. Main points extracted. Issues analysis. See how this works?"

Shepherd sniffles, "It doesn't have to be this way."

"Oh, Heathcliff, tell me how it's gonna be!" whimpers Hillary.

Shepherd says, "What about the pink?"

Mr. Drabble grunts out, "Pink prank." He whistles. "Did I lose you? We got off. Okay, a breather. What about the prank? A cool dada performance. Now we wait for the conclusion. The denouement. You never know when a performance will end."

We go on like this for a couple hours, adults coming over from time to time to remind us to use our 'indoor voices'. We go from the Enlightenment to the American Revolution to the A-bomb. We construct POV's, we offer analysis, we pretend we're acting like big kids. We bullet from the Great Dying to the horrors of colonialism. Mr. Drabble's tough and easy and sad and sleepy, and he appreciates our work. He loves to point out how the history of the law, or the history of economics, or the history of civil rights, seems to evolve in the same pattern physics does, or any of the sciences, from simple ideas of basic parts, or particles, to properties holding it all together, then new ideas, new properties, expanding, complicating, to annihilation. Evolution is deceptive. Imagine — compare, he says, the difference between a Dawn Horse and an Arabian stallion. America destroyed itself because it never would admit how its wealth was based on the misery of others, so too did atoms lead to weapons of mass destruction, the scientists reluctant to admit they knew their governments would weaponize their discoveries. It couldn't be stopped. The thrust of this information that no one spoke out, or offered a meaningful alternative, no one lifted a hand, fist to the sky (or not many). He ponders Neoliberalism and capitalism, the utopian promise of progress, then its crash, even though free markets are still obsessed over. We have a private prison economy in our state. It's the ultimate free market enterprise. What does it mean when a nation brags freedom but has more prisoners than any other country in the world? Contradictions. Interdictions. Intromissions. Now, Mr. Drabble gets all parental about the future, about the kinds of jobs the free market supports.

Finally, I go, "Why is it so weird around here? Pink stuff — whatever it is. Just kinda strange. Why here?"

Mona asks, "And what about the gorilla? Are there even any gorillas left on our planet? I want to know about the gorilla."

Silence. Mr. Drabble has pulled himself up, straightening his shoulders, head held high, ready to pounce. He leans in, over the table, in a flesh gush of head, nose, ears, shoulders, chest, arms and hands, then opens his mouth: "We're at the bottom of the page. Think of the map of the US. We're at the extremity. Hunker down place before consolidation. People ended up here. Before consolidation. Whatever that means. Does that make sense? I don't know what else to say right now. I'm sure Changing Woman has something to do with it. We're all bonkers, I guess." His sigh goes on too long and becomes contagious: everyone is tired now.

Time to call it quits. Time to get back to the semi-real—

Hillary mutters, "*Loco in de cabeza.*"

Tremaye says, "If humans are doomed, it would mean billions of years of evolution failed. Ergo: no way. Not the way nature works. Nature-evolution, learns from its fails. Goes on. It's part of the process. There's plenty of diversity, then options, selections, shifts. We're at the brink of one of those punctuated equilibrium dealios."

I go, "Or not."

Mona says, "If we live that long."

Shepherd says, "Population."

Hillary says, "Environmental disaster."

Mona says, "Genetic mistakes."

Tremayne says, "Fundamentalism."

Quentin says, "I-T."

Mr. Drabble pronounces, "My fellow clonedrones!"

Quentin exclaims the standard reply, "'I am not a number! I am a free man!'"

Mr. Drabble starts in again, "Here we are, at the bottom of the page, with a border wall that is no longer needed. We got water wars up in Phoenix and Las Vegas.

We got crop failure, famine, new tropical viruses. Since 1500 we could have fed everyone. Why didn't we? Your job, if you decide to take it, is to break this narrative arch, change it, spiral it."

Mona says, "Traitors of the Enlightenment."

Quentin says, "Sounds like the name of a band."

Mona says, "How many left-handed, how many brown eyes?"

Mr. Drabble squeals, "Don't look! Don't look!"

Mona figures, "You weren't going to tell us! It was a trick! Oh, what a web you weave! Tell! Count it off, comrades. Lefties? I know me and Mya are. No one else. See I intuited that. We all have brown eyes. Right, Mr. Trickster?"

Giggling and snorting, then we simmer down.

Everybody's checking phones before takeoff. I return the books I borrowed to Mr. Drabble. He says, "Good thinking today, Mya. You and Mona are regular rhetoricians. Stay with it. Take this one. Did you like the Eiseley?"

I take it. It's a fat, shredding paperback: *Zen and the Art of Motorcycle Maintenance.* "Thanks," I say.

Me and motorcycles. Sure. "Yeah, I liked Eiseley. He's a scientist deep in nature. He felt something older than himself, even though I guess he's an atheist. He seems like a lonely old man."

Mr. Drabble nods, says. "He's wondering what happened to humanity. But he recognizes that there is a humanity. It's a start." He snorts a laugh. It's an ugly sound. His phone squawks. "Shoot! I gotta run, guys! See you all next Tuesday. Happy New Year!"

Up and at 'em! He's gone. We stand and mill.

Quentin calls, "See you next year!"

Mona cries, "What about the gorilla?"

Tremayne mutters sourly, "I knew how many left handed there were, and what the eye colors were."

Mona says, "How? Share."

Hillary pushes in close to Tremayne. "What color are my eyes, Tremayne? No, don't peek. Now, now! Look into my eyes, young man! You are under my control now."

Tremayne looks like he's going to cry. He really doesn't know what to say or do. He reasons, "People use their favored hand the most."

Hillary steps back from him. "Clues! I'm tired of clues. All we do in patterns is look for clues."

Tremayne wanders off.

A kid our age, a big guy, comes over to see Quentin. They do a complicated handshake. He starts talking this party. A New Year's Eve party. He shyly glances around at the rest of us, and he says everybody's invited. It's gonna be at this vacant house in Saginaw. Hillary says those houses are haunted, but the guy and Quentin laugh. Everyone's wearing pink, says the guy. He takes off.

Hillary and Shepherd walk away together, talking. She puts her hat back on.

Quentin says, "You guys should totally come."

Mona looks at me. "If we can get a ride."

Quentin smiles. He zips up his jacket, gives a little wave. "Later!"

Mona and I stand close not saying anything. We adjust our packs and jackets. She says, "I can tell your you is not the you you usually you."

I don't say anything. I want to tell her.

"Okay, fine," says Mona. "I'm going over to the cafeteria. I need a stool or a small table."

I walk her over to the cafeteria, now kind of a dump where all the old stuff from the school — broken desks, chairs, lamps, stacks and stacks of computers — are piled up in teetering, decaying heaps. Everything covered in dust. Everything covered in spores. Kids are taking off. Adults rush by. It's still blue, though colder. Everywhere blue unnoticed. I feel Mona watching me. I know I'm being spacey, making her feel unwelcome.

As soon as we step in to the cafeteria — five more steps, now four, at that exact second, I will change channels. We step into the cafeteria. Door's open because a few other kids are scrounging around. A little boy is looking at a wall of old computer monitors. He can't be more than six or seven. He's sucking out ketchup packs. This is all he's knows, walls of junk and ketchup packets. That's a line. I tell it to Mona.

"'Ketchup packets' is crunchy, what it does to my mouth. Good girl," she beams.

We're looking over the graveyard of office supplies. Mona likes these rectangular metal stands, which, at first, we think are some kind of machine part, like some kind of mounting frames. Then Mona figures they're for organizing documents on a secretary's desk, her in and out boxes, Mona thinks, while the boss is playing grab ass. Mona tells the whole story, what she was wearing, how he lured her, all the way to the part where the girl gets pregnant and has a free, safe abortion down at the clinic.

"Yes," she decides, holding up a metal stand, "it's a little small but it should work." She turns it sideways, seeing how it'll work on its side.

"Computer skeletons," I yelp.

"Perfect — it'll be perfecto."

"What do you need it for?"

"I'm making a shrine to Tonantzin."

"Oh. This you is you all over my you. Just don't get distracted blah blah blah."

Mona giggles, slaps my arm. "Good catch, kemosabe. Hey, we don't work 'til next week. Training goes back regular on Tuesday. This is holiday. Poor people's holiday. Holiday without money. Still, it's *ours,* time to stretch, time to flee, time to pee. Only, I don't run like you do. I am allergic to extreme sports like track."

I'm laughing, can't stop. "How are you getting home?"

"For the party, we should make pink mud pies."

"Why?"

"To confuse the boys. They'll take one bite and be

under our control."

"Why would you want to control a boy?"

"They want to control us. They think we're amusement parks for their fun. You know, try out all the rides." She looks mean with squinty eyes, closed mouth.

Well, no, her lips don't look mean. When I tell her, her lips look like they are made of bubble gum butter, she says 'you just want to chew on them'.

She eases up, goes, "I gotta get the bus. Got any silver?" She opens her mouth. Her lips are chapped.

"Zinc." I give her my change, two quarters. Bus is whatever you got. I say, "I gotta go find Cecil. My ride. He texted me."

"See you later?"

"I can't wait to see your shrine."

"Don't hitch over. Your ma will get mad."

"I've never had any trouble."

We glare at each other a little while. We have to part ways.

Mona says, "Take a screwdriver." Her glare shifts deep: "You know you're gonna tell me."

"Stop."

"It's true, I've put a spell on you." She wiggles her fingers in front of my face. Each finger could be part of her new Medusa look.

"If you wanna know something, come with us on

our run. Maybe I'll show you something."

"Can I walk?"

"You seem to be able to."

Cecil knows all about the New Year's party. Everybody's going. Everyone in pink. The Painter. End of the world party! Lassies deep fried. He's so excited, until he realizes he's really stoned, and that makes him pfft deflate like a balloon, come down enough to concentrate on driving and slowing his babble. He says his boy, Delmont, knows the guy who found the house for the party. The guy's going all out: greatest border party in ever. Beer. Wax. Hash oil. Dub. Dew. And Delmont, a wacked DOG, got this idea, says Cecil. Delmont thinks we all should go in to old town in Coltrane, what's left of the touristy part, after midnight, and paint the town pink. Contingents have formed about how it should go down, and they are adamant. Cecil wants to paint the town pink.

"Where you getting the paint?"

"Pink stuff? I don't know."

Cecil turns in to his driveway, shuts off the car. We get out. I say, "Thanks for the ride."

He sways a little, says, "Do I smell like weed?" He pulls up his jeans, smoothes his t-shirt, poses.

I lean in to him, sniff. He smells like dirty socks

like most boys. "No," I go, "you smell like scorpion venom."

He laughs and hurries on in.

It's just a couple blocks to our house. Right here, these houses are vacant. Walk by watching my watching, keeping my keeping. Eyes all out, going everywhere. So called yards look like a war's come through, hardly anything left organic. Dust storm accumulation. The dust comes in from China, they say. It sifts in to the empty houses. No one sweeps up. What is dust? Platforms for spores! Dust whistles, when it flares in ghostly puffs. So, yes, everything is dust, and my mountains. Hello, again, we say together. I keep it open, thinking on how I felt with Mona.

I hear — bells?

The slump block house west of us, the next one down, is Ms. Cline and Hot Dog's. The slump block house right here, which is next to us on the east side is Crow's. He's an old Coltrane artist barely hanging on. Now, from his funk house comes a cascade of bells, chimes, gongs, pipes, like nothing I've ever heard before. Like put sounds together this way, and invent new sounds, messing around. What can we come up with?

I walk up to the front door, start knocking. I get in closer, my block head organ ear up to the hollow plastic door. Inside, nothing but gongs now. Outside, I knock harder. A weak voice calls out. I wiggle the door. It's unlocked. I open the door. No lights.

Crow's in the living room hanging from the ceiling by his leg brace contraption. I don't know what you call it. I get in to his view. He cries, "Turn it down! I didn't realize how loud it was until I'd already got set. I didn't want to have to come back down. Then I started liking it loud."

I go over to the entertainment center and find the CD controls. I turn down the volume. The flat screen TV next to it has a movie on, with Asians running in a field of tall grass. I've examined his exhibits extensively, so know his stuff, carefully presented from every surface — toys, minerals, artifacts. I know where everything is. (The tidal wave of Crow!) I am fumbling through the neighbor maze. I may be on his life planet. I hear my breath.

"Harry Partch," he says.

"Pretty."

"'Pretty'? Pretty wild? Pretty nutty, but 'pretty'? You're tired. You're worn and don't want to think. Okay."

"Harry Partch. I like his name. Bells and gongs, coming together. Yeah."

"Do you feel it?"

"Not as much, turned down."

"*Onibada.*"

"Wha-da-bada?"

"The name of the film." He gasps hard. Exhales long and carefully. He goes on: "This only works if you really let go of the spine. Release the Kraken! No, no. Release the chi! So I got that going on. The music, the film, I'm covered."

"What are you gonna do when you release?"

He giggles upside down. I don't want to watch his

chin. I start expecting his chin to be his forehead. He says, "I'm not opposed to delayed gratification. I'm not opposed at all. Just never tell people about the voices in your head."

I feel a bit dizzy, laughing, so adjust intake. Check the levels, watch my breathing. Laughing too hard in a space helmet knocks your head around. The way his eyes want to make his chin his nose. Disorienting. I could throw up. Which is the worst thing you can do in a space suit. I swim to a nearby wooden chair, drag it over. I drop my pack and sit in the chair.

"Good girl."

"You're the second person that said that to me today."

"You know why? It must have been someone close, a friend, like we are, who knows when you're tight, so I bet it was said like I did, when we felt you open to us?"

"I haven't seen my mom in a couple days."

He pauses. His eyes close. He whispers, "Done?"

"Can you see me nod?"

"I wish I had a cigarette."

"Can you smoke upside down?"

"Should we do an experiment?"

"I don't like to smoke, hurts my lungs."

"Do you want to know what I'm thinking?"

"Sure."

Crow inhales, exhales. "I mean besides wishing for a smoke? I'm wishing I could dance. I gnaw on that one like an old bone. Once you've tasted flight, all else flutters. I'm thinking about the piece I'm working on, *Monad.* I must dance the fabric of reality from a purely Dickian stance. And if not me, I'm picturing the perfect feet of young Asian women, dancing *Monad.*"

The music has settled, sounds almost traditional, like folk music. The shadowy house heaves a sigh. I come up for air.

He says, "Do you feel it?"

"That movie is weird, those ugly masks? Like monster heads?" I stay silent, but, at once, Crow, the movie, the music — how Crow it is. My parents like him. We eat dinner together about once a month. I like him though.

I know what's coming, and it does: "You're thrilled to be troubled, aren't you?"

"I feel dumb."

"I feel Kraken."

"How's your spine?"

"Very spinal."

"'Spill the beans'. That's what you're gonna say, what you wanna say."

"Beans? I feel like a grilled cheese sandwich."

"You don't look like a grilled cheese sandwich."

We both giggle, listen to this part of Partch.

I say, "Heard about the Painter?"

"Good song title."

"Some people in Naco saw animals covered in pink goo. Thick syrupy stuff. Pink rabbits, pink roadrunners. A lot of people have seen them."

"What kinds of rabbits? The ones with antlers?"

"I'm serious. Maybe one of your artist friends?"

Crow's mumbling. I don't like his name Crow. He's no Indian. Just a Coltrane dood. But he's been here a while. I don't understand what he's saying.

It sounds like, "Pink's a sacred color...punk's pink...here in the blast zone it can't miss...we work it...transformation...we pretend we're not getting dumber...disfigurement uncontrollable...dreams see things but they're not eyes."

"You're drifting. Crow. I'm not following."

He croaks, "Get me a drink of water."

I notice he has no water bottle near him. The Harry Partch seems to be dying. The film shows credits. It's over. I clamber over to his kitchen sink, adjusting my magnetic soles. There's a small glass to the side, near the edge, unbalanced. It could tip. The dirty dishes and forks and knives scattered about the sink are leaning, balancing, angling — precariously. Things could fall apart. It's hard with my space mitten to navigate the glass over to the jug of good water, then I have to lift the jug — no, first I have to unscrew the top, then lift it to pour. Why am I acting this way? I don't want anyone to get in trouble. But everyone will know when I take them there. We will discover it together. I take the glass of water back to

Crow.

He says, "You'll have to hold it for me. Wet my whistle."

I get down on my knees to do so. Water dribbles in to his nose. He splutters, "Too much!"

I leave the glass and return to my chair.

"Vigor," he says. "We're on a rampage, you and me. Spinal! I feel healthy, creative — no, wait, that's you. Not me. I'm going...to come down. Dismount."

"What are we rampaging about?"

"Aha! Not saying a word."

"Why are you talking like that?"

"Too New Agey?"

I snort. "Suppose the pink is poison. Or a disease."

"Probably."

"No one knows what to do."

He says, "Mya, born in the collapse, don't likee."

"I'd like to meet that poor girl and straighten her out."

"Are you going to stay to watch?"

"Do you need help?"

"No, not at all. I know it makes you queasy."

I leave Crow's place before he can discombobulate himself from the ceiling. He knows what he's doing. I think. I pause a second outside his door. No screams or cries of a bad disembarkation. I go on home.

Mom's old Datsun is in the driveway. Dad's not home yet.

I bustle into the house through the unlocked front door. I call, "Mom!"

She calls, "*Hija*!"

I follow her voice to the kitchen. She's sitting at the table holding a rag bulging with ice up to her face, to her eye.

She says, "You should see the other guy."

I drop my pack, hurry over to her. I lean in to wrap my arms around her.

"I'm okay."

"Let me see." I stand up straight.

She lowers the ice to reveal a nasty looking black eye.

"It looks like it hurts."

"It does."

"What happened/'

"It's a prison, *hija*."

"Oh, Mom." I hug her again.

"How are you?"

I murmur, "Good. We had Pattern Recognition today. Yesterday, I ran in the draw."

She brings the ice back to her eye. She's still in uniform, tight, starched clothes over her small body.

I coo to her, "You must be exhausted."

Chapter Four

It's so bright in here, the meeting room at the Naco Border Station lit up. Wednesday morning, after Christmas — let's do this! Skype's on. Somebody should draw the blinds. I'm sitting in the corner with my dunce cap on, low man on the totem pole. I'm on a spare chair, an old metal folding chair with dents as though it were used to bash skulls in. That kind of thing doesn't happen anymore. Not with the Sheriff's Department. Not with *La Migra*. We're goody goodies. Strictly defense. We're geared up now — a big deal. The bird cages stacked up at the other end of the room, past the flat screen with Skype on, are distracting. They stand for Sheriff Kang's most recent interdiction, in which I uncovered a safe house for illegal birds. It was ICE, Customs jurisdiction, but the birds were all dead so. Really nice cages, thought the sheriff. So he had them bleached and brought in. I guess hoping to sell? But, maybe, just as a monument to his on-the-job-ness. Couple people told him to get rid of the cages. They could have bird germs. That just made the sheriff certain he was doing the right thing. Whatever that might be. I can't tell. I may be the only Anglo in the room or on TV. Couple suits on Skype settling in, can't get a read on them. I know how this is going to go down. What should happen? Should. Should. Should be's. No matter how I imagine it going down the *right* way, by the book, it will go down totally mind fuck. Cluster fuck. I don't feel right about this. Maybe it's the glare lighting up the room, frying my cones and rods.

The suits on screen are ready. Everybody stares at each other. On my side of the screen, in front of me, the table my doods are sitting at, all in uniform, with their hands folded in front of themselves. They look like they're handcuffed. On Skype, the Grand Poobah hisself gets things going.

"Good afternoon. Thanks for being here. I'm Dr. Jose Herrera, Executive Secretary to Chief Medical Officer, Dr. Suzanne Barnard, of the Health Department, Homeland Security. I just happened to be in Tucson so. With me is Customs and Border Protection, Chief of Customs, Tucson Sector, Barack Sylvester. Please introduce yourselves."

"Chief Patrol Agent, Naco Sector, Jim Moros."

"Tony Gollan, Naco Port of Entry."

"I'm Sheriff Kang."

"Pat Patmos, Port of Entry, Naco, Sonora."

"Simon Silvia, Chief of Police, Naco, Sonora."

"Deputy Lucus Monroe. I'm back here."

Dr. Herrera says, "So, please, enlighten me this beautiful Arizona morning, there's been a leak? A spill? What's going on."

Sheriff Kang begins, "Two days ago, we had a series

of calls, seven in total, from the Naco area from people who'd seen animals covered in some kind of pink substance. Roadrunners. Cottontails. We thought it was a prank. Kids. Deputy Monroe checked it out. Saw no evidence of pink animals. Not a one.

"This morning, early, at dawn, Deputy Monroe was on patrol in the area again and decided to check out Greenbrush Draw. Since all the sightings were near there. That's where he found it." Sheriff Kang stopped.

Dr. Herrera doesn't smile, doesn't frown. He says, "Go on."

Sheriff Kang says, "I think Deputy Monroe can help us out here."

On Skype, the Customs guy next to Herrera, Sylvester, is kinda bent in over the table in front of them. He's one of those left handed writers that has to practically fold his upper body in to a pretzel over the paper to continue his furious writing. There he goes! Writing furiously down a legal pad, the long form, plus he seems to be stressed, bad vibes, sweating too much. Sweat drops on the yellow paper. Transcribing the meeting? Some kind of public penitent? Some kind of ceremony? Maybe their tape recorders ran out of batteries? A couple of our guys on this side have small notebooks out in front of themselves, but no one is taking notes. I think the sheriff is drawing curlicues like he does on his desk blotter. He's got the Skype controls by him. It's his show. Then I notice the way the light shines on the suits on Skype allows someone sitting off to the side and front, but out of view, to cast a shadow beyond Sylvester. Phantom mystery dood.

Dr. Herrera goes, "Can you sit up closer?"

"Can you hear me? I'm fine."

No response.

"I entered the draw this morning at 6:21 AM and proceeded up its middle, fairly open and clear, for about fifteen minutes. Heading north."

Dr. Herrera says, "What were you looking for?"

"I don't know. Trolling. Just looking around. Had a hunch, I guess."

"Go on."

"A mile plus into the draw I came on the pink."

"Pink? What was it?'

"Sheriff Kang, hit the pictures, please. They're from my phone, so not the best."

A photo takes over the flat screen in front of us. I assume the suits are looking at it too. A funky ditch photo, out in the desert, with one ditch wall side plastered in pink, then a pool of pink at the bottom. All pink. We get through most of the slides.

I come back with, "I don't know what it is. A huge amount was dumped from the eastern side of the draw, as you can see. I found tracks up there, above the ditch, truck tires, where the truck had backed in. There were also impressions in the ground by the tire tracks, round, deep. Like fifty gallon barrels would make, I'd guess."

"How much of the stuff?"

"Hard to say, your guesstimate is as good as mine. Hundreds of gallons. Maybe more."

Dr. Herrera says, "Gollan, did you have any unusual loads coming through lately in a big truck? Any chemical manifests?"

Gollan shrugs, then: "Nothing unusual. Our computers have been down. But none of our people noticed anything." Gollan talks in a shrug. He has no aura.

Again, Dr. Herrera speaks: "Chief Silvia, any talk of chemical imports, exports? Anything unusual on your side?"

Silvia's a tough fifty-year-old man whom I've had the privilege of working with. He's reliable. You can count on him in a jam. Like a battle buddy. "Nothing like that," he says.

Sheriff Kang says, "We got a sample to the lab. In Phoenix. They're pretty backed up. Could take a while."

Dr. Herrera says, "Does it smell? Did it make anybody sick? Are there any reports of anyone getting ill from being around this pink stuff? Deputy, did you have any affects from the pink stuff? You were close to it. Any sign at all of it being toxic — dangerous?"

I scratch my neck in two places. I pull my left ear lobe down. The pain isn't enough to bring me back. How can I eyeball it and know if it's safe? "Not that I could tell," I mumble. I have to decide what to say. "Slight smell maybe. Slightly sweet? It was drying up in the shallow spots. Places where it'd splashed to the side. The top surface of the pink ponds had caked up. Maybe a different color, more whitish, whitish pink."

On Skype, Customs dood, Sylvester, suddenly glances up, straightens up heroically. Man guy. Face, with dripping. The face parts with yellow eyes. I can see him now. He shakes his head as he asks, "No evidence of containers? Cases, bottles, buckets?"

I don't know what to say.

Fast, Sylvester says, "Industrial dump, an accident or on purpose." He shrugs.

Dr. Herrera says, "Sylvester brings up a good point. Jurisdiction. This doesn't seem to be a national security matter at all, though it did take place on the border. I mean, except in a very peripheral sense. Don't get me wrong: Homeland Security depends on your vigilance. We won't know what we got until the lab results. For now, cut it off, keep people away from there."

Sheriff Kang asks, "Who will pay?"

I venture, "Could be important — could be. No telling what that stuff is. So, just went by the book, if you're wondering why we called it in."

Dr. Herrera owns the meeting: "Of course. I'm glad you reported this. I want to know what's happening down here. Hopefully, nothing toxic. You said yourself no one seems to be getting sick. But there is the problem of a cleanup. You'll have to work on that."

Sheriff Kang goes, "Who do I call? State environment folks? Public health?"

Chief of Police Silvia says, "Suppose it could be paint?"

There's a pause. Quite an inhaled second. Because everybody feels guilty having wasted the suits' time, and it was me who pushed the sheriff to this high alert, calling up everybody. So down goes my bevel, and up goes my sucker, knowing I was doing the right thing means zilch. I get paid by tickets but nobody has any money.

I go, "One more thing. Pink animals. I saw them. By the dump site. Sheriff Kang, the next picture."

There's a noticeable exhalation: all along the desk and on screen, air's let out, shoulders come down, adrenaline's resorbed. I catch a flicker in a bird cage. But they are empty.

Still, no one wants to cross this road. Maybe, it is killing the animals.

I continue, "Pink rodents and birds."

Dr. Herrera asks, "Dead? Sick?"

"Hard to say. They were a mess. But I'm not a vet. Maybe we should bring the critters over to a vet to look at."

Dr. Herrera guffaws — I think you call it. "Paint would have killed them. Remember in *Goldfinger?*"

Sheriff Kang cuts the picture and we're back to Skype.

Sylvester chuckles too broadly and the chups become burps. Now they're playing me.

I say, "They looked bloated. I believe they'd been eating it. The pink. Really pigging out on it."

Dr. Herrera says, "Further proof it's not toxic."

Oh, yeah? Could be. Could be.

In 'stan we had a newbie come in who didn't understand the gas build up from MRE's. No one knows what they put in those sacks of pus. He'd get so bloated pigging out on them we'd have to sit on his stomach to force a release, or he'd be in pain all night, keeping us up. Radical fartectomy. Just thundering! Later, my VA counselor said maybe I'd come to this border region because it reminded me of *something* else. That's what she said. Not somewhere else. Something else. Like I came here to help folks fart? I wanted to laugh. I'd die for a good belly laugh. As though place was just a back drop, a drop cloth, an old table cloth tied up between backyard trees so Da could show home movies. That's an image from a movie. Maybe TV. Nothing like that ever happened to me. But I can't tell. Maybe it did. Maybe there are growing up, family fun images so common they've been embraced, and everybody shares these virtual tastes of how it might have been? We all watch the same movies. But *something else is somewhere-else-ness*: this isn't real desert any more than 'stan was. It's not a real ecosystem with plants and animals and a drip of water that manages to last eons in extreme brightness. Nope. Arizona, Afghanistan, here, there, these are blast zone leftovers, with sneaky opportunistic bushes here the same as those in 'stan. Lots of acacia, though they call them mesquite here. Used up places, raped and dried and drained and poisoned spaces. But *that* blast zone...in 'stan that blast zone much, much...louder... real blasts. So something. So somewhere.

Dr. Herrera holds up his right hand with fingers extended. He makes a fist. "In order of priority, likelihood of a threat, one — " He raises his thumb. "Kids. New Year's prank." He holds up his index finger. "Two. Illegal dumping of no concern. Yes, it's a mess. But the animals like it. You said so yourself. Three." He now has three fingers up. "Illegal dumping of toxic material. We'll find out ASAP. We have connections. We can speed up the process." He seems to nod to someone off screen, a secret transfer of favor. But I could be, I could be imagining the shadow man. "We have to make sure. Probably nothing. Make sure no kids get in to it. Four." Another finger goes up. "Deliberate contamination. More than vandalism but not necessarily terrorism. Eco-nuts? Environmentalists? Border activists? Making a point?" He shrugs elaborately. "Haven't seen much of those folks lately." All fingers are unfurled. "Five, terrorist act. And this is dangerous stuff, some kind of border action to cause harm."

Everybody nods happily. It's over.

Sheriff Kang says, "I'll see if the fire department has any water to clean it up. Still have to figure who's paying."

Sylvester says very evenly, "Alert. Abort. Anomaly. It's a frigging anomaly. 'A bit of spoiled potato.'" He's ready to go. He's ready to burst. These doods and their allusions.

Herrera smiles for the first time. Yeah, they're like a comedy team.

The shadow behind Sylvester gets tall, angles, turns, evaporates.

The bird cages smell. Doesn't that mean molecules of their leftover filth are making their way inside of me?

Chapter Five

I, Rigby Bishop, will never fight unfairly. I will look my partner in the eye and speak from the heart of power. Not my private heart, the heart of our family, a heart bigger than the sum of our parts. Him, me, Mona. A heart solid enough to be true to the biggest thing of all time: end of the world jeepers creepers. Yes, it is. It's the end of Western Civilization as the dominant paradigm. It's the end of capitalism. Everyone must be fed. Now they will be and/or it's over. We corpuscles, we tiny, tiny ephemeral dots make our stand for awareness, for family. For something to do.

Tom's standing in front of me. There are about thirty people bunching up, milling — we're in the middle, so pretty sweet chance of a good place in line. It's last Wednesday of the month in Naco, Sonora: the Compassion Center for Poor Gringos gives out a kilo of beans and a kilo of rice to each family in need. So we took a little morning hike from our house in Naco, Arizona...Naco, Sonora. Here we are. And I swear I am not going to bring up tortillas again.

It'd go like this:

Me: Make sure to ask for tortillas.

Tom: They have to offer them. No point in getting pushy.

M: Who's pushy?

T: Not me.

M: Maybe you don't hold your mouth right.

Unfair! Deliberately setting him up for my punch line. Tom's in a mood since it's a week from remittance. That's far, *far* away. Beans and rice until then. I'm not going to think about it. It's Wednesday morning, cool, bright. Should have slathered on the sun screen. The truck pulls up behind the building. We line up. You actually go in to the Compassion Center, when you're in the front of the line. One at a time. I've turned my back on our mountains, the Apaches, to face now into Mexico. Beyond the Compassion Center and the unloading truck, the only big building, with a warehouse, in Naco. The rest of Naco, both Naco's, one story wooden structures along empty streets. On our side, Naco's a hundred houses. A post office. A volunteer fire station. A defunct gas station/mechanic shop. Two dollar stores. And a port of entry, like the foundation stone, holding it all together. The little houses like barnacles around a living buoy. The intimate border. The Sierra Madres, just beyond Naco, in Sonora, at their northern limit, defined by Santiago Peak, what folks on this side call Blue Mountain, though it doesn't look blue to me. It's beige. Everything's beige. Beige is my favorite color by default. I remember before Mona. Tom and I were in Geneva, for a big tech confab. The famous mountains around Geneva were pretty, sparkly. I guess people thought of them as majestic and serene. For some reason, Tom and I found them oppressive: official beauty. They were too pretty, too much sparkle. They were hulks clawing the sky. We knew they could crash and fall. Was that when we knew we had to go? Assumed beauty had become assumed defiance. The big world mountains threatened sinister. We knew what would happen. A few years before the meltdown, we retired. We were young. Here, our mountains are barely holding up the sky. Sky so bright! Blue bathes pure.

Tom's head turns and gives me a grim look. He's tall and thin, with a long neck, so his head swivels like a bird. He likes me to rub his neck. Chicken neck. He's all I got. And Mona. This way it is. No use pondering if it will get better. We're too old now. Our decisions play out right here. We wanted to simplify, a simple existence. Why does simple end up meaning poor? Such a cliché. Vagabonds. Hippies! Nouveau pauvre. Dot com boom and out before the crash. We're on sabbatical. Forever. Sedona seemed right. But too expensive. At the bottom of the map, where you couldn't go much farther, Coltrane. Coltrane, like spiritual boot camp. Coltrane was small enough. Mona was born. Naco, Arizona was just right. Home now. No car. Take the bus. Simplify: simplified. Keeping it clear and clean. Getting by like two old monks watching the moment. Because it *is* bright. The mountains now.

Tom's body, the whole tall drink of water, comes around. He takes the step to me. He bends in close. I smell incense.

He whispers, "The people already served our leaving with tortillas. They have tortillas."

I smile. He smiles. He gives me a little peck on the lips. Blue gets on.

The thousand dollar binoculars are better than my other pairs, but I always have to treat them so carefully, like a fine china cup I could breathe on funny and break. From here, top floor office of our border trucking operation, the windows give a view to the north, in to Naco, Arizona. If it weren't for the line of cormorants at the Compassion Center, it would be empty. Not cormorants: distaff Americans in gray plumage. My scan takes me along the border wall. I'm looking for black throated sparrows, one of my favorites, a very handsome bird. The 10 x 50's are great for this kind of scan. I've often seen them out around the wall in the brush. The wall only goes for a bit on either side of the Naco Port of Entry. It never got finished, no one cares. The birding here is nothing like it is at the rancho. There are so few birds left around here. Hermosillo is far enough away to be in a different watershed. Our rancho is twenty minutes out from the city, in hills that green up in the monsoon, with a year round pond, water all year round. So birds all year round. Out here not a drop. Naco used to be a hot spot of smuggling and illegal immigration. Now it's a truck stop? But it's Wednesday, and the churros deal went through smooth as glass. Life is good. Ha!

Abuelo Estrigeno was jefe for this entire part of Sonora. Those were the bad ol' days of weapons, torture, murder. It's as different now from those days, as those days were different from pioneer days, when our people first came to the Chichimeca. Back in the day, there was more water, but there were also Apaches, and militant landlords who ruled with a gun. Maybe Abuelo's world wasn't that different. Now, out here, for a birdwatcher it's tough. Bright sky over brown mountains should mean nothing can hide. But sightings have slumped. America's shit leftovers laid out before me. This is where America shits itself, all the righteous fools, melting to *mocos*. Species disappearing, gone. Migrations, weak. In Hermosillo, me and the family can hold out a long time. If we have to. Let it blow over. People are moving away from the border country, heading south to the cities. Consolidation even here — it's just starting. Everyone wants to start over. The whole world is trying to start over.

At Brown, we used the old classic, *Cycles of Conquest* by Ed Spicer. It's pragmatic, yet the pattern, or model, of cycles works. First, the Indians show up, of diverse backgrounds and interests, and they take turns bossing each other around. The Spanish show up, but it's pretty hard making a living here without the help of the locals, so lo and behold, the birth of a new people, the Mexicans. Mexicans take over, but they've had things stacked against them, and they have a civil war. Finally, the gringos appear — how long will they last? We're about to find out. Cycles. The cosmic race takes its place.

Look at the line of people coming to Mexico for a hand out. Shabby Americans, mainly skinny, with bad skin and funky hair, in line for rice and beans. The desperate. Americans are leaving, too, for Tucson consolidation. But, right now, these seedy, deranged Americans, who's ever left, come for rice and beans.

I lower my binoculars when I hear the door open — no knock. I turn and there's Eddy, my chief of operations. He used to work for my father, before we went totally legit. He grunts at me, nods slightly. He's wiry, small, but tough. Dark skin, short hair. Not as old as my father would be, but close enough. He's got a nice cowboy shirt on, jeans, beautiful cowboy boots.

"You see the check for the churros?" he asks.

"Sure," I say. "Nothing to retire on. But easy money. We're good. Things panned out for us."

Eddy doesn't like it. It eats at him how we've...evolved. I can tell he's going for it today. He comes closer, standing near the front of the desk. I unwrap the binoculars' strap from around my neck, place them on the desk carefully. I sit at the desk's big chair. I feel like a kid in the adult's chair. "Sit," I say.

Eddy keeps standing. He pffts. His hands are in his back pockets.

"What?"

"That's just it."

"What are we talking about?"

"Easy money? Living check to check. Getting by on churros! Gimme a break."

"How many times we had this conversation?"

"Easy money." He shrugs, lets out a whoosh of air. "Marco, Marco."

"It's safe."

"It is."

"So?"

"What if I got a deal wrapped up? For sure, we're safe, but we stretch our boundaries. See what I mean? Safeness, with a helluva lot of profit." He finishes. He says quietly, "One more time."

"I don't want to know."

"You won't have to know. Pick up like usual, by our regular truck guy. He crosses the border. Delivery to the dollar store guy, Señor Dinero. Just the same. No surprises."

I wish I was at the rancho, hanging with the fam, going on nature hikes, mornings for birds, evenings for constellations. We are so cozy. How — why would I do anything to threaten that?

"What's the catch?"

"No catch." Eddy's left-handed, and his left hand comes out of his jean pocket and he raises it to about gut level, where he indicates what he needs with a flick of his finger. His index finger flicks back and forth. I pass him pen and paper.

He pulls the pen and paper close, gets the pen positioned properly in his left hand, and leans over the desk, beginning to write. I can't see what he's writing, but the movement of his hand suggests a lot of loops or circles, a lot of zeroes. I would say they are zeroes, or suns. He's drawing multiple suns over the desert landscape. One of those days when it's killer hot and bright, multiple suns scorching the Earth. Sun in every direction! He pushes the page to me.

I whisper, "Wha — you think we're bugged? You think we should have the room scanned for bugs."

He shakes, his left hand splashing out to indicate I should pick up the sheet of paper. He lets out, "That's it.

Look! Take a look!"

I look. "Lots of zeroes. I knew it."

"Those zeroes should be ours. Pick up here. Cross the border. Over to Señor Dinero. That's it!"

"You said, 'that's it', rather emphatically. What's up? You don't think we have to have the room scanned?"

"College boy! We're so legit now, we don't have to worry about bugs. We got no drones flying up our ass. No cops on us. We are squeaky clean. That's what we're selling."

"A guarantee."

"Exactly."

"It'd only work once."

"Maybe a couple times."

"I knew you were — "

"This once! One time."

Both of us glance elsewhere, walls and ceiling, but definitely away, avoiding each other's eyes.

He goes, "Tiny bit of risk." He shrugs, steps back.

"Drugs?"

"No."

"Weapons?"

"No."

"I don't want to know."

"Marco, listen, I don't know either. I don't care. What does it matter? Once the truck's over the border, we're done."

That's a lot of zeroes, I'm thinking. "We'd use Ted? The usual?"

"I'll call him right now."

"Whoa! You already set it up! For right now?"

I committed the family to the straight life. I can't go back on my word. For years now, Eddy's been pushing for us to expand operations.

Eddy's pacing in front of the desk. His hands are back in his pockets. It's a couple steps either way, back and forth, a simple dance. He stops, exhales, goes, "Now's the time. Why wait? What's to wait for? This one time. Chance of a lifetime. They're right here."

"Who?"

All those zeroes...

"The guy."

"Who is he?"

"How should I know? He knew we did trucking. He knew Señor Dinero. He came to me."

"You don't know him?"

He shakes his head.

"Seen him around?"

He shakes some more.

"Mexican?"

"How should I know? I didn't ask for his ID."

One time.

"It'll go down this afternoon? Tonight?"

"I gotta call Ted."

"Your guy, this guy wants to meet me?"

"He knew your name, the family name. Word gets out, you know. To cinch the deal, a handshake."

Enough zeroes, I could take the whole family to Tucson for our very own birding festival! It would be super fun. The kids would love it. If it's open, we could go to the zoo. We could live it up.

"Bring him on in."

Eddy is all smiles and nodding, with a bobbing head. He turns from the desk — whoosh, and out the door in a flash.

I sit there looking at my thousand dollar binoculars.

Eddy returns with a man. He's taller than Eddy. He's dark, hairy. Looks tough. Scraggly beard, long hair, small eyes. White t-shirt and jeans, battered sneakers. He's ugly. I don't like him right away.

I stand up.

They are in front of the desk.

The guy goes, "We load the goods in your truck, I give Eddy the money. Half of it. Your truck crosses to the other side, makes delivery to the dollar store guy, who gives you the other half. Simple. Deal." He nods.

I nod.

He puts out his dirty hand. I take it. We shake. It's a worker's hand, callused and rough.

We keep nodding.

Our hands break apart.

Eddy leads him away. I haven't said a word.

Eddy returns in a dynamite minute. He's jumpy, full of it. Happier than I've seen him in a while.

"Easy money, Marco. I'll call Ted. He gets his truck over here. We're done."

"Who are these guys? How many are there?"

"I don't know. Who cares?"

"He looks like an Arab."

Eddy grunts. "We all look alike, jefe."

"What're the goods?"

"I don't know. I don't care. They need a truck. They need some kind of guarantee, no questions asked. We fill the bill."

"One time."

"I should go call — "

"But I don't get it. The border's open. What is it about this load they're being so careful about? And the zeroes? Come on, way too much — "

"They gotta get their stuff across the line. They figure with us no chance of a screw up. Easy as pie."

"You make it sound — "

"Easy money."

"It's too much money."

Chapter Six

"That's what it said! 'I hate myself'. And if you ever tell anyone I said such a thing, or told you anything about it, I will deny it and run you over with my truck some night you're drunk and staggering home along Hereford Road. Hector, we're not friends. You work for me. I pay you so you have to be my friend. You have to listen. We're celebrating! Churros all the way, dood. But let me finish my story. So my ma got the rocks and minerals bug — everyone does when they first get to the border country. Everyone falls in love with turquoise and malachite and azurite. People sleep with their heads surrounded by azurite. Don't ask me! Supposed to be good for your dreams. But that shit even back in the day was expensive. So Ma ended up mainly collecting agates. Quartz. All like that. Those silicon minerals? Lots of silicon all over the Earth. You know what chalcedony is? Kind of milky quartz? Real soft and cuddly, like you just wanna finger it. Used to make coffins of it. Agates have these impurities, different stuff, I don't know, like chemicals, that give them color. Story rocks? She loved those rocks. Stories built in. She'd rub 'em all day long. For her, the choicest ones were this peachy orange color — carnelian. She thought they were the best. She got this notion up her butt that if you leave carnelian outside, the sun will bake it, cook it, I don't know, make it darken, bring out new shapes and colors. She thought a message would emerge, like a sign. So she did it. Left her carnelian outside in the sun. And that's what came out. That's what it said, in tiny black hen scratch. I could read it plain as day: 'I hate myself.' That's what it said."

Hector says, "You think I live on Hereford Road?"

"Man, that's what you got from my story? Message from the sun, dood! I am fucked! It is ordained." I gasp for special effects, clam, almost fart. "I'm baring my soul to you, my comrade at arms, as we celebrate our churro glory, and that's your 'tude?"

"You drank the whole pint of Old Crow. Didn't even offer me a sip. Slugged that sucker down. We finished the sixer. And it's not even afternoon. We should eat."

"You're the boss."

I lunge out of my patio folding chair. I'm up.

Holding, holding. Navigating. "Hey, you're the one who had to get home last night. No time to party."

"I knew you only partied on Wednesday's."

Grim dim, flim flam, dark in the Cave. I call it the Cave on account of the bats. On account of the cave grubbing apes around here. It's because of the broken action figures all over the place. It makes sense: Cave...bat cave...of parts...toy parts. It could be a meme. A dynamite action *telenovela*. Crawling with dirty little limbs. Action figures are a polite term for toys, but big he-men cannot be seen cavorting with the He-Man toy, so we changed the name to *action figures.* That's a lie, but it's all lies. Splattered heads, crushed torsos, broken legs, joints askew, and all with waving hands. They're always waving. Toys are our friends. Well, when you're a kid play is important, maybe the most important thing. Play offers life, enjoyment, even when the hard scrabble is going down. Before virtual reality, we already had full psychic immersion. Inside my own head, this fricking potentiality for fun and adventure. But I don't collect them. I save them. They're like landmarks, buoys...in the Cave.

The Cave's in Coltrane's warehouse district in the Bakersfield area. They're all empty. Abandoned. Who would know? Who would check? Creepy warehouses like Coltrane's elephant graveyard. Don't want to attract attention. But long before Hector, I staked out my claim. Kept it careful, watched the lights, activity on the down low. No one must see. No one must know. Dark as a cave. I laugh. They laugh. My cohorts. My hordes. My little toy chunks, reverberating with the good times of some kid. Life's a see saw — regular life, then dreamy play life, illustrated with action figures. We go up and down, back and forth. Like me on one see saw seat and the other seat loaded with littles, trying to see saw me up, up high.

Action figures don't search for their missing pieces. I'm the one picking up the pieces. They sure aren't collectibles. They're junk scrounging turned up. Bitten, broken, battered, from little girls' pony stuff, to all the superheroes that come and go. I don't do it for fun. It's a filthy habit. At the edge of the parking lot at the dollar store will be a Hydra ninja without a head. Maybe some dood pissed on it. I don't care.

The Cave is secure, the warehouse graveyard right

outside, with hidden parking for the truck. Plus, easy access to a power line a buddy tied onto, plus he did the cable. Here in the Cave, glimmerings! Cable TV, computer access, lights. All for a couple cases of Mexican Slim Jims that fell off the back of a truck in a delivery. Boom. I'm set. Hidden. Safe. No one cares. The Cave is one big space. Private sleeping area in the corner with shades. I'm discreet. Entertainment center. My work table for action figure rehabilitation. I tried rebuilding them, repainting them. I'm shitty at it. Strictly rehab.

Now what was I doing? I move to the fridge, open the top freezer part. The freezer is full of frozen meals. Gotta watch what I eat. Traded for a crate of these bad boys. I pull six out of the freezer, at random. Hector don't care. He'll eat two. I get four. I hate myself for being a slave to my feeds. Cause that's what they are. I feed at the trough. Lies. All lies. Laugh out loud. I'm safe. Hector is my partner. For me, in the Cave it's all about the routine. I only drink one day a week — Wednesday. I smoke smash one day a week — Friday. Routine keeps the crazies at bay. Maybe they're next door, peeking. Friday has always been my favorite day of the week no matter what Hector thinks. Teasing me about it. Who's he think he is? What's wrong with him? How long we been together? On Friday's I like to look at Jeopardy MILF Porn, my favorite — mountains of ripeness, milky white boobs, real women.

Hector says, "You back?"

"Well, sure."

"You heard about the Painter?"

"Painter?" I shake it out.

"I heard from some people. Sheriff's wondering what's going on."

"What's going on?"

"Pink animals."

"You said it was harmless. An element."

"The Painter's like a New Year's prickle of life in a dead corner of planet Earth."

"There you go! Who's drunk? Every time you talk that way I'm gonna say *who's drink*. Who's drunk! Just like that."

"What are you going to do with those frozen meals?"

"I'm trying to put 'em in. The microwave. One at a time. It's how it has to be! That's all it can do. Then we eat."

"Are you expecting company?"

"They're diet, you gotta do two or three, at least, to fill up."

I sidestep a poorly positioned space heater buzzing angry red and head for the shelf with the microwave. One at a time. I put down five next to a broken sander. Nothing will jump off the sander to the white cardboard boxes of the frozen meals. I know how to do this. Some kind of dirty frogmen have to be pushed aside, their flippers streaked with red. The microwave is pre-set. Now Hector's giving me a look — patient horror. He hates me. *That boy's gonna be the death of me!* I mutter. Whoa! Did I say that out loud? Segue! Segue! Have to keep him guessing!

I don't think he noticed.

Go on: I open the box, slide out the meal, scan the directions upside down. I've had practice though to read them like this. I tear open a corner, put it in the microwave, which has red splatters like from gunshot wounds. Close the door, perfect fit. Hit the button.

Hector says, "Well done. What about the barrels? They safe here for now?"

"The barrels. We clean 'em up, put 'em on the market. We kill. Make uh fricking killing. Nobody comes over here. You think they're gonna be stole? Do you have a cigarette? They're safe. Here. For now. Hit the button."

Hector says, "You don't wanna talk bidness."

"Exactly."

Ding!

I open the microwave and slide out the tiny tray, push it to the side. It's hot. Duh. And I get the next one in. Unpeel its corner. Close the door — click.

"Did I ever tell you how I got the truck?"

"The bank's truck?"

"Don't. Never mind."

"What's your favorite horror movie?"

I can see Hector has a bashed in Stinkor in one hand. Where's She-Ra? My favorite all time is Martian Manhunter. Hector's trying to placate —

"I see! Humor the drunk until it dings. *Jaws.*"

"*Jaws* isn't a horror movie. It's a monster movie."

"My stomach!" I grab on to the belly meat and groan and fart and belch.

"You gonna throw up?"

Ding.

I manage to straighten, get the job done. Number three.

"Okay, what's your favorite monster?"

I hold up my hand to count, can't remember how. Then:

"One. Ymir from *20 Million Miles From Earth*. John Carpenter's *The Thing*. *Hellboy I* and *II*."

"Those aren't monsters, those are whole movies."

Ding.

I go for number four, shout, "The cyclops in the *7th Voyage of Sinbad*. That's a perfect monster."

My phone rings. It's in my jacket pocket, tossed over a chair. Must have left it on. Dumb. How late is it? It's early. We're just gonna eat. I'm not gonna throw up.

"You gonna get that?"

"Easy as pie." I turn from the shelf with the microwave, its soldiers lined up to be devoured. Hector gets up, stands up.

"I'll take over the microwave," he says.

I get to my jacket, pull out the phone. Push. Raise it to my face. "Yeah."

"Ted?"

"Yeah."

"You know who this is?"

"Eddy?"

"Don't say my name!"

"You said mine."

"It's your phone, jefe."

"I know."

"What're you doing?"

"Celebrating churro day."

"Nice. How would you like to make some serious *dinero*, but it's gotta be right now, no questions asked? Pick up here, cross the line, to the dollar store guy. You know what I mean? Just like always."

"More churros."

"Don't worry about it. It's safe. Think of it as an emergency order. You'd be helping us out."

"How much?"

"Three zeroes."

"When?"

"Right now."

"I know where you are?"

"Then." He hangs up.

I can tell he nodded there after saying 'then'. Eddy's okay. I think he's okay. He's a Mexican dood through and through. Just like I'm a fat pig dood who is about to savage a Lean Cuisine like a fiend.

Hector says, "What's up? You got all serious. Sobered your ass right the hell up."

"Let's eat. Then. We got a little gig. Hey, it's Wednesday. Two gigs — one, two, right after each other, one after the other. We gotta roll. We'll eat, and I need water. I'm not sick. I just gotta dehydrate." I dig in.

"Hydrate?"

I slurp, "What were we talking about?"

"What are we talking about?"

"That was my Mexican guy in Naco."

"Yeah."

"He's got an emergency job but it's gotta be right now, no questions asked."

I can see Hector sober up like a naked girl bathing in the spring when she realizes someone is watching. Will he exhale? Will he fart? Will he blow?

Hector does a little pfft like a baby spit. "Ted, how many times the Mexican guy or Mr. Dollar use the expression, 'no questions asked'?"

"How do you mean?" I manage between inhaling two Lean Cuisines at once.

"How many times?"

We've been together years. Peas in a pod. You

scratch my back, I'll scratch yours. No, Hector hasn't been with me that long. I go, "Never."

"What are we picking up?"

"We? We picking up? They load it there, they unload it here. Who said anything about needing a we?"

"Now you're being petulant."

"You start talking like that, you know what I'm gonna say."

Hector finishes his first meal. He lays the plastic fork down. "Aren't you a little bit curious about what it might be? I got to know I can get home to my place on Hereford Road tonight. Know what I mean? We done okay, because we done it clean."

"Nobody said anything about the unclean."

"This isn't a monster movie."

"Who's drunk?"

"I know that."

"People making fun of my figures. I don't collect them. I pick 'em up when I happen to see one. You know, driving around, in the trash. They're gross. Pure funk. I'll see Mum-Ra sticking out from under a dumpster. Maybe a skunk's been chewing on him. Know what I mean?"

"You know what we're picking up? He didn't say, did he?"

"You're assuming the worst. Don't do that. Don't assume the worst. It's probably Fig Newtons! Right? Expired Ramen. Stale pretzels."

"Can you drive?"

"What do you mean? Course I can drive."

"Whew. This is — " He shovels in cuisine. "Tasty."

"Quit complaining. Two gigs — bam, bam, man! We're on a roll!"

Addendum
Intermission
Interregnum

Wednesday is no nothing day

No one could ever understand —

Where's Mona?

Who's Mona?

I'll go over to see the shrine.

She'll go: "Glad you could make it."

I'll go: "For you, everything."

She'll go: "Breathless, are we, sweet pea?"

Filth is free time paralyzed

FREE TIME ANALYZED

What is this thing called 'out-of-it'? So-called 'out-of-it' days, or moments, are the fog of Wednesday, one day stretched out, day off for good behavior, an all out day noticed lost. Can't be riled. Can't be interested. Can't be indulged. Teens seem to wallow like hippopotami. Hippopotami in the watershed, but there is no watershed. I'm frozen on the go. Whipped to a palsy frenzy. Hippo modus operandi. Stretched sublime.

How long can giant ground sloths go without water? They must get water from the leaves they munch? No leaves! What is this thing of seeing what is not there? All times overlap. Giant ground sloths still here hair, their reverberations go on, meet mine, how do you do, together in the Earth crack.

I watched 2001 again. I've seen it ten times. I turned off my phone and concentrated. Watching as though my life depended on it. Guerrilla gorilla, vapor tapir. Spaceship Orion. I know places around here that could be the very same Luna lunar moon surface. I sat in the chair before the monitor, feet pulled up, books across my knees, and I began to study. I checked my essay notes. Labor Unrest and the End of Capitalism — 21st Century Style! Dribble says you can't put an exclamation point in a title. When the notes are clear enough, the piece writes itself. I'm almost there! Tonantzin in space!

Where's Mona? What's she doing?

I'll hitch over.

She'll go: "Thought you'd never make it."

I'll go: "Told you I would."

She'll go: "Shall we dance?"

We dance!

I wonder about Dribble's gorilla in the room that we were not taking account of. Context. It's always an emergency. It's always a time of change. Guess the magic phraseology and win a prize!

Our context is dust mud.

I dip into my motorcycle book from Dribble, just when Spaceman is in the French bedroom and knocks over the crystal goblet.

By afternoon, I write a text: 'Nothing happened on Wednesday, Mona. I was out of it. See you tomorrow, yes?'

(Do not send.)

Chapter Seven

When I wake up on Thursday morning, I'm running in my sleep in my bed like a dog on its side, arms and legs pummeling the covers. There is no memory of intercalary chapters, but I am aware of that, because I am flitting awareness over all things. I fall back asleep. When I wake up the second time, I'm on Mars, Mexican Mars, and I'm in a space habitat like a Mexican restaurant, gaudy Aztec calendar by the cash register, colorful place mats, fun armadillo bowls for chips and salsa. The sharp metallic tang of oxygen in the air. Changing Woman sits across from me in a high-backed chair. A big orange chair. She has a slight smile on her tough face, staring at me. She's not pretty or ugly, she's — my feet and legs release in a spasm. Cliché! I ain't dreaming that shit! It's a joke. It's a riff. I scatter back and forth, conscious, sleep, then conscious sleep.

Anybody can dream. Imagery is a trap because it's fricking commercial. Predictable. Ploy play. I need a dream that is so new, only I can fill it. I was playing in my dream. Like I was playing in the arroyo. I guess that situation still…tasks me. Why do I only consider dreams when I am dreaming? Because I have to go with the flow. Grown up stuff happens. Work for the night is coming. Not everybody was a hippo or a hippy, but all our parents are *be-here-now* addicts, like baby Buddha bozos. That's how they cope. Easy peasy mysticism requires the leap of faith to explain. I don't want to believe.

Dream kilter. Adjust. Shift. Sift. Hello, me. Hello, you. Hello, me you.

I wake in the air because I live in the air. I live in my bed, which is a boat. My hand climbs up my throat to a piece of tape. I recall a thorn. I'm too goofy to get up. My cells squeegee spastic plastic fandango. Shivers, yawns, shimmers. My molecules give each other high fives. Alive again. Alive another day. Like I'm stoned. A tingly feeling. Cells, behave! Feel sleepy alive, my muscles, my limbs, arms and legs, feet and hands, can't stop curling, curling. There are all these places to situate. Tonantzin on Mars. Blast zone. Pink place. Mona. She's a place. So random. What I got here is a stalagmite. What I have here is I see what I can't see. Half asleep, half awake. Pink dreamscape. Clot cleaners! What should I be doing? Hauling ass! All depends on what *be, here, now* refer to. They're like the three scoop banana split I never had, but plenty of images available. There are so many *be's,* so many *here's,* so many *now's.* Sometimes, I come out of it: this is a diorama of beauty in the 21st Century, me all stretched out under the covers in my underwear. I am languid getting up. How perfect loose ends jingle. Reel it in. No Peggy. No Testing paper due today. La de da. I grab the old paperback on the end table next to my bed. It's the one Dribble loaned me.

Cycles. Spirals.

I'll read it yesterday.

Last night, pink. Pink everywhere. Mouse came by last night, Dad's old buddy. They grew up together. He pops in occasionally, and if Dad is alive, not conked out, they drink a few beers and have a few laughs. He's called Mouse because he's big as a house. Always comes bearing gifts. This time a bunch of those plastic woven shopping bags you get in Mexico, filled to the brim. One bag held Tecate. Another had carrots and a small leaky bag of soy sauce. The last had homemade Mexican cheese — still wet and crumbly, and *masa* (Yeah, right, as if Mom ever has time to make tortillas. I don't know how. I hope Mom slept through the visit last night.). I transferred the liquid to a glass jar as carefully as I could, to whoops of laughter from Mouse and Dad. Supplies. No questions asked. They went out the sliding glass door to the little back porch to drink their beers. Sometimes Mouse brings these hand rolled Mexican cigars. Not last night. I made popcorn for everybody with soy sauce and hot sauce. Super yummy. I was sitting there pigging out, watching *Sleepless in Seattle* for the zillioneth time, t-shirt and gym pants, bare feet, when my energy flared, and I couldn't sit still, started flexing my feet until they hurt. I grabbed the big bowl and went out back to join them. They'd already finished their bowl, so were glad to see me. They were talking about the Painter and laughing. Mouse handed me a Tecate. Dad didn't seem to notice. Dad was saying something about 'pink elephants'.

Mouse shoveled in popcorn and burbled, "Pink roadrunners — yeah, I'd like to see that."

I didn't want them to see me shaking. I managed, in between chugging beer — so good after all that popcorn, to say, "Could be toxic."

Dad snorted. "Toxic — we would have heard by now."

"How you figure?" asked Mouse.

"The feds'd be all over it," said Dad.

Mouse spluttered, inhaling a great handful of popcorn, and said, "The Painter, man. It's a kids' thing. Right, *hija*? The pink? The pink!"

A huge burp came bubbling out of my depths startling the men. I pretended to scan for the empty desert highway in the distance. I knew it was there. They were quiet a complete second. Then they both burst out laughing. I jumped, stumbled right into Mouse, but instantly deflected myself in to a handy ocotillo, our squid-like death trap masquerading as a yard plant. Ocotillo emerge from the desert in long, snaky arms covered with sharps. Usually eight or ten arms. I've counted them. But Mouse caught me, pulled me back in time. Just a nick, said Dad and went to get a piece of tape. It was dark, he couldn't see very well.

One beer and I surrendered. I read, or pretended to, until I crashed. *Zen and the Art of Motorcycle Maintenance* turned out to be about taking care of your stuff. If you're fastidious with your motorcycle, it'll keep on keeping on. Like those motivational posters at Testing with a kitty that read, 'don't fret the small stuff'. So what's the big stuff? Peggy. I don't know about motorcycles. But I'm liking the book, its long dense sentences. Its slowness to include the boy. I hold the book in front of myself, waking up, getting oriented.

I didn't dream about the book or Mouse or my cut. I dreamt about running and Changing Woman.

There's something in the world beyond words. Blast

zone knowledge hurts on cactus hooks. The desert floor sparkly, ground into the caliche. Trash world. Blast zone requires it.

AYADEMYAVICHY

Makes me think of Abracadabra. A magic word.

My guts gurgle.

What language has those 'ya's'? Probably pretty common.

I better get up. Check on Mom. Check my phone. What time is it? Don't look!

Pink intrusion — and when we go for our run, they'll know. Everyone'll know and ask me if I know any more about it.

The Painter did it.

At the mirror, I peel off the tape and look. The scratch on my neck is gross, canoe shaped. Maybe a kayak. Like a tiny, sideways mouth, full of parasites. I could throw up. No, it's like a little vag — on an otherwise splendid neck. Some cultures worship women with long necks. I look so girly. Society demands bypass. Peroxide! I'll clean it, tape it. The mirror takes my breath and makes it fog. I pull back from the sink. My neck isn't that long. Since I woke, I been scratching, itching around my wound. Wrong. Clean it. Don't touch it. I can't stand here at the sink forever. My hair is a luxurious nest today.

Cecil gives Mona a ride over. That's interesting. Wonder how that worked. Cecil's mom must still be on sick call, unless the bank's closed. Donna's mom drops her off. Mona's closed up. Weird. WTF. We're standing in front of my house, grimly idling, when Will and Otis show up in Otis' old beater. That's four runners. Not bad. Ms. Winter will be glad to hear it. The whole team gets together for official practices at the church. Usually, there's seven of us. We're not really a team, more of a club. Donna's small but fast as a gazelle. Will is the tallest boy I know, or have ever seen. His short wiry hair and small round head give him a look straight out of the cantina in *Star Wars*. Actually, he's been ordered by his parole office to take part in community activities — like track. When he runs, he looks like a heron or something, but he's got stamina, makes it to the end every time. Otis is seventeen, so the oldest. He doesn't say a lot but he's strong, in pretty good shape. Running's like his hobby. He likes to say he's worked since he was five. That's how come he's got his own sweet ride. Four runners and one walker, Mona. Mona has her hair back, big boots, tiny backpack. She's in jeans and her steampunky jacket. Everyone else's in gym pants and sweat shirts, with running shoes, plus the mandatory backpack.

Mona spits out, "Cut yourself shaving?"

My hand goes to my throat. (Thorn duty.)

Otis says, "How far we going?" He starts warming up.

Will stands there with his elbows out, like armatures

for wings.

It's not that cold, maybe in the 50s. Donna and I start stretching. Uh-ho, here come Hot Dog and Spike, curious about festivities in the hood.

I point to the dogs and go, "Trouble. We better get this road on the show."

Mona shrieks, "Hold on! Don't be hasty. Geesh, you guys. Give a girl a second to get ready for adventure. And if one of you trips and falls, I ain't stopping to pick you up."

I'm glaring at her. She makes a face back, but goes on, "You guys haven't heard, have you? Not a one of you checked your phone this morning. Girl, you haven't been on at all."

"So?"

The dogs sniff around our feet but not too crazy.

Donna says, "What happened? What are you talking about?"

Mona says, "Last night at the dollar store on the highway, the one about a mile from here, there was a shootout. Police, Sheriff, State Police, all over the place."

Otis says, "I thought there were a lot out. Will, didn't I say that?"

Will says, "He did. We drove right by there. Was anybody killed? Was it a robbery?"

Mona says, "Nobody knows. They're not saying. They're figuring gangs, I guess. They're not telling."

Will says, "Gangs? You gotta be kidding."

Donna says, "Was anyone killed?'

Mona shrugs. "Don't know."

Will says, "Who knows what's going on? We gotta open border, hardly anyone around, who knows how many shootouts go down without anyone even finding out?"

Otis grunts. I guess in agreement. I think, if a shootout goes down and no one's around to hear it...does it pink? Smothered in pink...

Mona slays with, "Fuck it! It's New Year's Eve tomorrow, and there's gonna be the mother of all parties—"

Will finishes: "In Saginaw."

I say, "You been talking to Cecil."

Mona smiles wickedly. She looks like a cat.

Donna comes over to my side. "Can I use your bathroom?"

Otis and Will groan. They look like giant mantids.

Mona says, "She's got to go to the bathroom. Don't be asses."

I say, "Sure," and turn to walk her in to the house. At the front door, she whispers to me, "Do you have any tampons?"

"I'm not sure. Maybe Mona does." I call for Mona. The boys groan again. Mona gives them the finger and hurries over.

She yells, "Girl talk!" And to us in a spooky whisper, "'By the pricking of my thumbs,' and all that jazz."

We go inside. I explain. Mona goes, "No way! Me, too. Started this morning."

I feel a flash, a flush. A gut clench walks in and kicks me in the belly button. We all head for the bathroom.

When we come out, the boys are sitting in the driveway with the goofy dogs in their laps. The dogs have big satisfied grins as though they've won, or proven something. We resume our stretches, watch our breathing. Now the dogs get annoyed and start barking. Little pops and pips at first, but the intensity grows. It's time to focus on the stations to Greenbrush Draw.

Mona says, "They feel how giddy we are. Shootout. Giant party. The Painter. End of the year, man. Giddy up, mi gente! You'll be my charioteers, riding me out into the infinite desert of tears."

I go, "That was good, Mona-groan-a."

Will says, "Whatever you're smoking, I want some."

"No you don't!" spits Mona. She's like a fucking raptor.

I feel like a girl. If I don't take off now, I won't, or I'll collapse, or I'll burst into a thousand baby spiders.

The four of us run. We go slow, watching the dogs, feeling it out, tensing, relaxing, getting in to gear.

Mona calls behind us, "Don't wait up!"

Will mumbles in between gasps, "What's her trip?"

Donna goes fast, "She's cool," then Donna goes real fast, peeling away from us, to the end of the road, where she turns left, heading to our spot to enter Greenbrush Draw.

Mona yells, 'Giddy up!'

Otis calls over his shoulder, as he's moving ahead, "I ain't waiting for her!"

Will and I pick up our paces. Hot Dog and Spike are behind us now, so the lingering barks must be for Mona. I can imagine the jokes she's telling the dogs. Donna's up ahead, already waiting by the culvert where we go in. She's running in place, going around in circles, then stopping to stretch and bend. Otis gives a whoop and hustles by her, down the bank, in to Greenbrush Draw.

Donna smiles big to Will and me as we come up to her. She whoops, "Feeling good!" She's outta here!

A bunch of mutant pigeons flutters by in a splurge of lice, right over us. I hear a question mark, maybe a thrasher. This is the place to go down. These are mi gente. A high pitched, two note call sounds. The coyote bush by the culvert has orange eyes, watching us humans whooping it up. Will and I go down the bank, into Greenbrush Draw. The blast zone opens up, wonders what's going down. I will not puke. I'm fine.

We're all spread out, hitting our strides. Otis is gone, out of sight. Donna is ahead of the rest of us. Me, then

Will. Mona is somewhere behind us. The walls of the draw refuse to let us anywhere but right down the center. We take it careful, pass chunks of trunks. Tree trunk stumps, involved chumps. Tree trunks' multiplex apartment complexes. Where I've been. I have a kind of internal map of the whole arroyo. Tobacco trees. Sumac. Some mesquite. Cottonwood hulks. Messy! It's all zooming by. Quickly, I see a bunch of tiny moving parts in those Italian bushes that have gone wild and clogged up the draws. Maybe, Fae. The import makes a ton of seeds and little guys pig out.

Behind me, Will's making noises, huffs and puffs, then extra f/x. Loogy power. I'm taking it easy. Feel good — strong. I can do this forever. Right down the center, capped by blue, clear sky. I can tell Donna's slowing down, then farther up I see Otis checking out the bottleneck of brush that I had to get help pushing through. I slow down for Will.

We admire the toaster and old timey telephone, hanging in the debris, pushed to the sides now. It's a narrow spot between tall banks. It was clogged shut.

Will and Otis want to know how I got through. When I don't answer right away, they check their phones. No one's brought water but me. So what's in the backpacks? I pass around my plastic water bottle. Donna's not breathing hard at all. She smiles as she drinks. I think she's feeling good. Otis eats some beef jerky he has in his pack. He also has a Dr. Pepper in there I see, but he must be saving it for later. Will's red-faced, thin lips, sweat beading his forehead.

I say, "I had to clear this out the other day to get through. I needed all the help I could get."

"Check it out," says Will. He's put his phone away

and picked up a stick. He stabs the long, thin stick at a thick branch caught in the messy tangle of the bottleneck. "Looks like a deformed arm. That old grass and scuzz could be hair. It's like the arm of a monster."

"It's a fucking branch," says Otis. "You're seeing things."

Donna goes, "Why hallucinate when reality is so nice."

We all look at her.

"Let's get going," says Otis, finishing my water, tossing the empty back to me. I have one more bottle.

Will says, "Wait, wait, wait. I want to hear what Donna has to say. Don't you think the Painter's a stoner?"

Donna chirps, shrugs, starts stretching in an open area of sand. She's getting in to it. Then she stops and looks serious. She goes, "I've never been high."

Will starts, "Then, how do you — "

Donna pushes in: "We know where this is going." She laughs. "I mean getting high — it's turning away from the world." She holds her arms out, fingers spread. "Away from this. This is okay. Let's run!"

Will says, "Donna Pardo, you're high on Jesus or something. That's okay. I don't care. We been running all this year and I didn't know you were so deep."

"I need glasses," says Donna. "I can't see deep, barely close."

Will says, "Me, too. I need glasses to look at you again, Donna Pardo."

Otis says, "I need glasses, too."

Donna says, "I need to go to the dentist. But I'm afraid."

I say, "I've been to the dentist. I don't like it either. No matter what they say, it always hurts."

"Shit," says Otis, 'yeah. Least you guys have indoor plumbing. I am so sick of our outhouse."

Donna says, "Spiders?"

"Black widows," groans Otis. "I hate 'em!"

"Wait a sec," says Will. "Am I hearing things? Do you hear something?"

"Oh, my," goes Donna turning, then pointing behind us.

Here comes Mona singing a song.

She's singing 'Kill The Poor', and she's at that part where Jello Biafra screeches, 'kill, kill, kill, kill, kill the poor; kill, kill, kill, kill, kill the poor'!"

Donna's waving.

Otis says, "I'm going on."

Will says, "She might have more water."

"Eh, I already drank hers." Otis takes off.

Mona calls, "Scared off the big dood?"

"No," answers Donna, "we've finished our break. We're gonna keep going. Mona, you got color in your cheeks!"

Will and I snort polite chuckles. Will says, "What, you think she's a zombie?"

"Of course not! Hi, Mona!" Donna's waving! "I'm going on. We'll visit later."

Donna assumes the position — stretching.

Mona has joined us now. No more singing. She swings her little pack around, so she can get out her water. "Donna, have a drink before you go."

Donna falls out of running stance. "Maybe a sip. Thanks." She takes a sip. Lots of smiles beam from her, then they float out like jellyfish pinning themselves to our faces, all these good vibes slobbering our heads with politeness. Donna says, "I don't think the Painter is a stoner. I think it was an accident. If it was a joke, then at the party tomorrow totally pink, right? Everybody'll be pink. Just remember not to paint that square in the lower back so you can breathe. I saw that in *Goldfinger.*" Donna takes off running.

Will says, "A couple of things come to mind. Is Donna Pardo going to the party tomorrow? What kind of accident is she talking about? Maybe Donna's the Painter? Can you imagine Donna Pardo watching *Goldfinger* with her family, and they get to the part with the female pilots and their leader is Pussy Galore?"

"A glorious name," says Mona right away.

"Donna has a glow about her today," I say. "She's a normal, healthy monster."

"Whatever that means," says Will. "Is she into Jebus?"

I shrug.

Mona says, "This is the spot where you had to use your secret super powers to part the trash like Moses at the Red Sea."

Will says, "You're tripping, man."

I laugh. "Mona knows all my secrets. You do have color in your cheeks, *chica*, like you just had a feeding. Do you need to sit down, put your feet up?"

"I like it down here. Arroyos are cracks. Crack in the Earth! When the walls are high and the crack is narrow, it's like being in this capillary of the desert. Oxygen! I need oxygen. We're too deep. I feel like — we're wandering the dank desert lungs."

"Blood metaphors again," I say.

Mona says, "You started it!"

Will says, "The desert has lungs? This is a dump, man. Leftovers. The backwash. You guys are creepy. I mean I know you think I'm creepy, but duh."

Mona says, "I don't think you're creepy. Either does Mya. I came along to keep the monsters at bay."

"What monsters?"

"Tell him, Mya."

"*Pequinos, duendes, la llorona.*"

Will shakes his head. "I don't speak Mexican. You guys are freaking me out a little, but not in a bad way, I mean I like you, but now I must be going. I'm going, you guys! Don't get behind, Mya. You're gonna eat my dust. See you later, smashed per-tater!" The tall stork sloops or stoops, or storks, away, high shinned, huffing and puffing at once.

I go, "What do you see?"

"Mya, don't do that. You know — geez, I'm not sure I like the way you're looking at me. Your course. Your crack."

"I'm glad you're here. You'll see. All secrets will be revealed. Meet you at the end, mashed per-tater."

I decide not to take the patrol car all the way to the edge of Greenbrush Draw where the pink stuff got dumped. Park back here. I want to look around. I'm off duty, so technically not supposed to be taking out the patrol car, but uniformed or not, I gotta air out. It's quiet here. Brush and sand — and dust. Whole world is dust. Deputy Lucas Monroe been up all night on dust duty, assisting with the dollar store incident. Hours with the sheriff trying to get a picture of what happened, like even a timetable. How many shots were fired? How many people were in the little truck, the big truck? We couldn't figure it. Stories didn't match up. Witnesses demanded to be paid. There were jurisdiction issues: who would pay for the investigation? When the big boys showed up, all authoritative, like we were rubes, we knew they would not be sharing. But they would be covering costs. Finally, at dawn's early light, I brought up my point to the sheriff, that maybe there was a connection between the pink stuff in the draw and the dollar store incident. He just looked at me, the famous thousand yard stare. We didn't even know if there had been any fatalities. All we knew was a lot of bullets had been fired last night at the dollar place, and no one saw a thing. So, my impertinence was beyond the beyond, and he told me go home, with all the windows rolled down in the patrol car to air out my *cabeza.* "Yes, sir, Sheriff Kang!"

It's going round and round in my head.

I gotta clear my head.

Greenbrush Draw right there. I could spit in it.

Way too many feds for this to be a simple, locals shoot out. Taking it to the next level then. Gangs make no sense. A stupid cover. At least, we know whose truck it is, the big one. Cashier ID'ed it for sure to us and the Coltrane police before the *federales* showed up. That's a given now. The old man who owns the dollar store, who defended it with his handy dandy Browning 1911 .45, claims to be in shock, so whatever. He doesn't seem to know anything about it, anyway. Protecting his property, 2nd Amendment — his story. He's not talking. The feds had guys with fancy equipment going over the parking lot. Which means what? Hidden treasure?

I get out, close the door, leisurely walk over. Odd pink spot.

The old truck tracks are melting away. Wadda we got here? New truck tracks (same vehicle obviously), pretty fresh, hours old I'd say. Less than a day. This time the truck must have backed around without pulling up to the edge like before. They were turning around, I figure. What the hell were they doing back here?

I have to get down in the draw and see if anything new's been tossed in.

The same truck from the dollar store incident. Why not? But why would they come back? Koontz, the guy who owns the truck — I think I met him, one of those slobby, lardbelly guys, is in the middle of this. What has Koontz gotten himself into?

Right up my spine heat climbs. I'm being watched. Close. I don't look. I don't change expressions. My heart doesn't even beat fast. I can feel the space between us. I know where he's located. It's like the land around me makes a mock up in my head. I know where everything is. Where I can dodge. Where I can find cover.

Now a voice comes in over my preoccupation: "They're coming."

"Who's coming?"

"They're coming."

"Show yourself."

A dark blue suit man, good looking, good shoes, my age, comes out of the brush. We look at each other. I never could tie a good tie. This dood's got it down.

"We don't have much time," he says. "We already met. On Skype? I was the shadow that only you noticed."

"How do you know that? How do you know no one else noticed?"

"Your tone, different from the others. The way you talked." He makes a micro-shrug. "It meant you were on."

"FBI? Homeland?"

"Sure. Whatever. But listen: kids, from around here, they're almost here. We have to get to cover."

We hustle over to some brush at the edge of Greenbrush Draw. But it's mesquite, the nasty thorny stuff. Everything in the desert fights back. Sends out whips to rend the flesh. We get down on our knees. I go to my butt so I can scoot over to the edge. We're to the side of the dump site where the truck parked. Maybe I can smell it. Maybe I smell FBI. Finally, I glance over the edge. It looks different. It's drying up, white-pink crud layer on top of pink puddles.

I whisper, "Tests come back?"

"Usual screw up. We may need more samples." He's got a device out, like a computer stick, and he's leaning out, taking pictures with it. I think. He comes back, arranges his body in the thorns. Amazing, he hasn't ripped his suit to shreds. "What do you know about this Koontz?" I shrug, so he goes on, "Guy regularly crosses the line for the dollar store."

"Oh, yeah. That is interesting."

He raises his left hand to point up the draw, to the north. A big guy in sweats comes jogging down the center, where there's a vague path. As soon as he sees the pink, he stops. Big guy, maybe Hispanic, brown hair, maybe 6' 2," 190 pounds. His eyes get big. Mouth open like a fish.

He gulps, gets out his phone, emits a startled, "No way!" He does that all at once. Then he yelps: "Gotta take some pictures. Get 'em out there!" He manipulates his phone and gets close to the pink. He takes a few pictures.

"No way!" he shouts, and takes off running back the way he came. He's shouting ahead, "You guys! You guys! You won't believe this shit!"

My battle buddy took pictures. He glances at me, grimaces, says, "Part 1 — the Discovery."

"It means he didn't do it."

"Maybe."

"I gotta get down there, check it out."

"Well, not right now."

"No."

He looks at me funny. "What are you doing here? Oh, I get it: sheriff deputy goes rogue. You had a hunch, no one listening, you came out here because — finish the sentence, please."

"Because last night's dollar store truck was the same one that dumped this pink shit."

"So random. Good hunch."

"No coincidence. With what you say about Koontz, we can figure he was hauling something from Mexico?"

"Here they come."

We watch as the big guy triumphantly parades back into sight, this time with a small teen girl that couldn't have weighed more than seventy-five pounds. Cute, blond, pixy face. She, too, in sweats. The guy ushers her to the pink.

Her response pops out: "Oh!" Her hands come up to cover her mouth. Then she's covering her nose. "I don't want to breathe pink." She backs up.

The boy says, "Take a picture of me by the pink, in front of the pinkest part."

"No! Too gross!"

A big whoop sounds from where they came from. A real character comes plodding in to view, huge feet, giant sneaks, in sweats. Looks retarded, with a too small head. Maybe a few inches shy of seven feet. He takes in the pink, standing still, surveying. Can't tell much from his face. No startled expressions like the others had. Suddenly, he hurries forward, shoveling hands flapping, and says, "Don't you get it? It's Mya! Mya did it! She knew about it. That's why we're running here today."

"That don't make no sense," says the big guy. "We always do practice runs out here."

The girl says, "Why would Mya do it? It's an industrial accident. I read about them. That's what it is. An industrial accident. It was in one of our pamphlets. We shouldn't get too close. Could be pink fumes."

Tall boys says, "What are you talking about? You see any industry out here? You still don't get it. This is where the animals got pink. It must be."

The girl says, "The Painter did it."

Tall boy goes, "Of course he did. It makes sense. But turns out he's a she."

A second girl runs in, stops abruptly. She's tall, slim, dark hair pulled back. Multi-racial? Or Hispanic too? Looks healthy. She gasps, her eyes glancing over her friends' faces, then she's wildly looking around. Everywhere. We duck. She's looking for us. She spots us easy.

"She's sharp," whispers my buddy. "I'd like to get a picture of her. Mya."

"Let's go down and talk to them. No big deal. Why not."

The small, younger girl says, "Mya, you look like you saw a ghost."

Mya says, "It could be dangerous. Don't touch it."

"It's Pepto! Duh! Gimme a break!" says the tall kid. "Mya's all warning and advice now. When she lured us here in the first place!"

Mya says, "What are you talking about?"

Tall guy's a bit agitated. He goes, "Donna, Painter's not an industrial accident. Come on! This shit's drying up. It's done. The biggest party of all time will have to do without this shit. I know: we go *in* pink, wear nothing but pink clothes."

"I wasn't going to paint myself pink," says the girl called Donna.

The big guy says, "Take my picture in front of it! Come on, somebody." He's pleading, and no one seems to care or be listening to him. He gets belligerent: "I ain't wearing no pink! Girls wear shirts and pants with that word, 'pink', written right on it. What the hell does that even mean? Why do girls wear that shit?"

The tall boy says, "It's obvious what it means. Donna, all we gotta do is *wear* pink. Like clothes. Masks! Pink masks! Giant pink rat masks! Yeah! And Mya will be queen of the biggest party ever. Queen of the pink! Saginaw will shake! And Mona will die of jealousy."

A third girl comes stomping in. This one is dark haired, pale skin. She's not as small as Donna. She immediately looks angry and calls out with a big voice,

"I'm always dying of jealousy of my little tortilla chip." Then: "Holy moly, roly poly, guacamole! Pink! It's here! Pink! Pink! This is where it happened."

"She's tripping," says the tall one.

FBI guy backs up on his butt, stands when he can. I do the same, hardly scratched at all.

The new girl notices us first and whoops and points. They turn to look at us. We walk to the edge, look around for a place to get down.

FBI guy says, "Hey, you guys, know a good place to get down?"

The new girl says, "Why you want to do that?"

He says, "Just to talk. Just talk."

The big guy yells, "Cops!" and he is gone, racing off the way they came.

The tall guy says, "Hey, no offense. But that's my ride." He takes off, long limbs negotiating like stilts.

I find a place and we scoot down. It will be hell getting back up. We both swat at our clothes, knocking off the dust and debris. His suit has lost its sheen. My filth blends in. Then we walk to the three girls who are studying our every move.

The new girl takes over right away: "Welcome, Surface Men! We are Crack People. No, not that kind of crack. And not the kind plumbers with big bellies and low jeans love to exhibit. If you know what I mean."

FBI guy says, "Duly noted. Thanks. What a mess!" He's walking around the dried up puddles, looking it over very carefully.

Donna cries, "Gross!"

I say, "Those guys — "

Donna pipes in, "We're the track team from Sacred Heart. They're on the team. We're on a practice run. They had to get back. That's all."

FBI guy says, "No problem. Can you believe this? Who would do such a thing? And what the heck is it?"

The new girl, Mona, lets us have it: "Whoa! It's coming together! The great juggling jigsaw puzzle of non-TV life! All the pieces fall into place." She raises her hand for Mya to slap, but Mya leaves her hanging. "Mya!" she says.

Mya stares at me and the FBI guy with piercing eyes. She looks angry, too.

Mona goes, "Don't you get it? The reason these guys are out here after the shootout last night is the pink is connected to what happened last night. Regular Sherlock-a Holmes, doods. Don't be jealous! Sometimes a person's just got it."

The FBI guy gets all red in his ruggedly handsome face. But he's quiet. The girl scares him.

I got his back: "Come on, kids did this! Right? I bet you know who, too." I go from one set of girl eyes to another. They are choice. They are brimming over in their looking. I can see they are —

"Layers, man," says Mona, shaking her head. "Layers upon layers here. Layers of watching. Who watches the watchers? Who watches those watchers?"

FBI guy says, "No coincidence."

Mya says, "What do you guys want? Who's paying for this? All this law enforcement!"

The FBI guys says, "Sure. Whatever. Routine — we were checking it out. Saw you. Thought we'd ask what you know."

Mona says, "'By the pricking of my thumbs — "

Donna says, "I gotta get back. My mom's coming to get me."

I say, "Fine. We're trying to find out what this is. How it got here."

Mona says, "For our own good. Because it could be dangerous."

The FBI guy says, "You're one step ahead every time. Have you ever thought about a career in law enforcement?"

Mya says fast, "She's very good at enhanced interrogation."

Mona calls, "Go ahead, Donna. We're right behind you."

Donna says, "I'm not afraid." She bursts in to a run. She's gone!

Me and the guy hedge, flounder, hesitate like total losers. Finally, I go, "Okay, then. Be careful."

The guy says 'later' and we head up the draw to look for a place to get up. We find a spot where the wall's collapsed. Head back to our vehicles. I go with him over to where he parked, not far from me.

I say, "Now what?"

"Why do girls, even little girls, wear pants with 'pink' on them?"

"I never thought about it."

"You don't have kids?"

"Uh-uh."

"What's Saginaw?"

"Back in the mining days, wherever there was a shaft, a cluster of houses would grow up by it, all these scattered neighborhoods with their own names, like Saginaw."

"Going to the party tomorrow night?"

"We practically were invited."

"They're not involved. They live around here. Still— "

He gets in his car, a nice looking, dark Camry with only a few mesquite scratches.

"Don't I get a card or something?"

He smiles. "We've never met. We did not do this."

"Who the hell were those guys?" wails Mona.

I'm piddling in some offal. She giggles when she peeks. She tosses a stick into a puddle. She's looking for clues like a regular telescope. I finish, stand, fix my pants, manage a shrug, and: "We should get back."

"The others have gone home by now. We should go over to my place."

"One thing at a time. It smells funny."

"I don't think it can kill you."

I declaim: "Makes you stronger!"

She snorts, can't resist, then, fast: "Who were those guys?"

"Did you think they were here to kill us because we know too much?"

"I'll kill you!"

She dives for me but I am faster and duck and twist aside, grabbing the middle finger of her right hand. I bend it back till she swoons. I let go. She grabs me, her arms going around me, her hands locking behind me. She holds my arms down with all her might. I bend my head into her head, tangle heads, push her head. She pushes back. We break, gasping battering rams. Sighs, pants, slacks —

I squiggle, "The figure is a seductive one."

"What do you see? What did you see? How did this come to be? Tell me!"

"There are faces — "

"Still — "

"Un autre."

"Overlap."

"Overlap?"

"Yes, overlap. When we're close, on the very same page as Dribble says, we know what's real."

"Heavy. Smart."

"Mya, we both know you're smarter than me."

"You're sexier than me."

"Earth loves tall girls." She shatters, backs away dramatically, arms outstretched. "Girl, the crack weeps for pink."

"The crack isn't — Earth weeps for its children."

Mona growls, looks around. Her eyes take mine. "Now we're acting on purpose?"

"Eyes of the unexpected! Suddenly, we have a mystery. What we thought was a prank and/or art show turns out to be deadly. I could tell you tales that would freeze thy young bone. Anyway, who's going to pay for all this law enforcement?"

"Tell me!"

I nod and nod, hop away. I'm a bunny. I'm a hop toad.

I go, "What if a giant ground sloth showed up?"

"Go on."

"What if I saw a truck back up and dump this shit?"

Mona goes, "I am so turned on right now. You are

revealing! You are revealing too much to the world, my little tortilla chip. But, you know, all these agencies. Something's cooking." She's unsure how to proceed. "What do...pink puddles...pink poodles...have to do with a shootout? Why do people have shootouts?"

I hop: "According to TV? War is constant, violence."

She hops: "Space wars, bug wars, magic wars. Zombies, vampires, plagues."

I stop. "What do we know?" I let out a long gasp, then start twirling. I go round and round Mona.

She says, "I'm seriouser — "

"Merry-go-round, merry-go-round!" I stop to catch my breath and laugh. "When things're crazy stupid, superheroes save the day."

"They're like angels."

"Violence freaks."

"All men do is kill each other."

"They can't stop killing each other."

"Everyone's got PTSD."

"I've got a pink sweatshirt. You can borrow my pink jacket."

"For tomorrow? You wanna go?"

The voice calls from behind us, to the south, where we have been making a point not to look, so we instantly jump. Full stop. The voice is creaky, raspy, and goes like this: "Who watches the watchers?"

Mona jerks around fast. "Ah, the pink show continues!"

Mona stuns well.

She crams her water into her pack. Gets her pack back in place. She's scanning to the south like me. It's all brush, broken scrap, stumps and trunks. Mona spies a long stick by her feet, its tip in the pink. She scuttles down to grab it up: pink held high. She yells, "Who goes there?"

The gnarly voice strains to be heard: "It is I, Tiresias, the blind wandering oracle. Is it safe to come out?"

Mona looks at me. I look at her. She thumps her stick on the ground. "Behold!" she cries. "The crack has given up its ghost. Welcome, ghost!"

A raggedy old guy with a back pack walks out of the brush. He doesn't look like his voice. He looks like one of the old hippies you see in Naco getting handouts. I can tell by the way he moves that he may look old and funky, but he's tough. Skin polished natty brown. He walks with confidence, slightly limpy confidence. He has an open face not nearly as gnarly as his voice. Big eyes on us. He isn't blind!

Mona cries, "He ain't blind!" She thumps and thumps her pink tipped stick.

The man asks, "Do you know what an oracle is?"

I go in to Wiki mode, reading from the dump: "The coracle is a small round water vessel with a wicker frame covered in hides used by the ancient Celts of Britain."

He's all smiles. "You are so funny. Maybe the funniest person ever. Right this moment in all the world no one else thought of that superposition. Now is in front of anything else, everything is out front.

"You were giving me a show. You thought I was more law enforcement. You were trying to bewitch them."

Mona says, "You're telling our fortune? You came out of the crack to tell us the future?"

He turns to Mona. He sells her a smile. He's kind of pushy. "You're funny, too."

Who are these people?

Mona groans, "Not a question. Special forces, right? Grandpa secret ops? We saw the movie! Watchers! Watchers watching. All these peeps in our crack. I don't know why everyone is so into atoms, I mean duh: they make up everything."

I insert timely, "Do you know about the pink? The shootout?"

He goes, "Right on. Not a thing." But no smile. The open face has to try to stay open. His voice isn't so rough close up. He looks tired. Beat.

It must be going on noon. Maybe the high sun propels this moment, these ducky visitors. I remember what I overheard from the pink guys. Put that with what I heard the cops just now talking. Now this guy? How do these guys fit? Something rotten has crept in. Maybe we are being spotlighted to majesty. I am relying on Mona to high noon us out of here, away from this watcher.

He edges around the pink stuff, getting close, pulling back. "Pink!" he cries. Then: "Who's this Painter? You guys know about this?"

Mona swallows her tentacles, says, "You saw the whole thing."

"Not a question."

"You're coming in from Mexico." She holds her stick with two hands now, pink up.

"Not a question."

"Port of Entry's too hot right now, so you figured you'd walk in."

"To my own country."

I say, "You've been living in Mexico. All those refugees down there."

He nods, smiles. He exhales and the voice comes out less raspy, but sad. Not sad, wistful: "Lived in Coltrane a long time ago. Wondered about it. Had a dream about it." A different voice now. Dreamy empathy. Maybe each voice is a different character. Isn't that what happens to oracles?

"Were we in your dream?" asks Mona.

Now the fellow wrinkles up his face, scratches his nose. He's got one of those old Army jackets on, green Army pants, big boots. Now he looks like a sad old soldier. Different character.

Do we all do that? If I try different voices —

He says, "Of course," but softly. Then: "I knew you were up to something. That something big was happening."

Mona tries a different voice, oracular, querying,

"That word? What's that word? Predestination? No, that's not it, about telling the future, all like that?"

I say, "Prestidigitation?"

His laugh is a pink phlegmy bruise. He says, "I don't do tricks. Not this oracle coracle." He stops, breathes. Like he's going to cry. He goes on, "I've been away a long time. I always liked it here in the winter. One day it's sunny and bright like spring. The next day it's cold and drizzly. Very dramatic. I know the ol' U-S of A is not doing well. You hear a lot of stories in Mexico. Mexican Net loves to detail conspiracies."

Mona tries, "It was the lizard people!"

"Fracking, fucking, fapping tilted the axis," I say, smirky, fast, suddenly lightening up, but still wanting to foil the fortune teller. He's a time traveler. These interlopers! Some kind of release bubbles up, making me go up on my tip toes. I want to run back. I want to get away from the pink. I say, "Prognostication."

He goes, "Ahh."

Mona says, "You were here when Coltrane was hot."

"In the 80s and 90s, a lot of artists ended up in Coltrane. It's at the bottom of the page, as folks around here like to say. Nowhere else to go. We knew what was coming. We thought we could hide out and make our tiny magic in peace."

"Did you?"

"Hmmm?"

"Make your tiny magic in peace?"

We keep looking at each other, going from face to face. I guess he's so aware of the old ways, the old days, it's a heaviness in him. Maybe that's why he thinks he's blind. Pink's a shit magnet. Faces and forces pile up. When we face the pink. He walks over to the pink again, nudges at some pink rocks with the toe of his boot.

He says, "You know the suit was probably a fed. The other guy, a local. You know him? Is he a good guy?"

Mona says, "What does it matter? We weren't doing anything. We didn't do it."

He warns, "But you're all on their radar now. Probably got pictures of you. Always best to stay under the radar."

"Mya, got that? No radar. He's gotta point, Mya, this blind dood. See it?"

I go, "I think pink emanations cloud our rods and cones, so that drone facial recognition probes will not be able to crack the Crack People. Not that kind of crack."

He gushes, "You're the funniest people in the world. I think. Right now, by this pink, in this crack in the Earth, and you are in it, on it, of it, spokespersons, MC's, Earth roadies. You would have loved an all night Grateful Dead concert. My generation, we were always visiting, passing through. My whole generation was just passing through. Hanging out. Waiting for the next thing."

Mona says, "See, we can't figure out that kind of poetry. Unless it's our fortune? Like in a fortune cookie? You don't look Chinese?"

I cry, "Tell us the future!"

"Light and dark. Light for a while, then dark for a

while."

Mona and I look at each other and burst out laughing.

He cries, "You guys are too much."

Mona says, "You should meet my parents. You probably know them. They been in Coltrane since the olden days."

I say, "My neighbor was an old town artist. Before he moved out by us. Goes by Crow."

Chapter Eight

I told Gershon he was on duty. Deal. Man up. Protect the fucking border. Or me, Tony Gollan, would kick his ass. This is my port of entry, so I'll be in my office. Better not disturb me. Wednesday night for crying out loud. Me here until at least midnight. Who cares? It's bad enough having to take this shift, but having to work with a dumb ass makes it perfect.

I lock the door, go to my desk. I get the computer booted. Go where I want. Until the screen is filled with delectable, triumphant Hentai hero/heroine, Esmeralda/Ezra. Quite a novelty, I think. I can't get over how you can find anything —

Blinking red light.

Not a good sign.

I'll ignore it. Put a piece of electric tape over it.

The desk phone rings.

I pick up the phone.

Gershon goes, "Inspector Gollan?"

"Who the hell else would it be?"

"I have a glitch."

"What do you mean?"

"Radiation monitor went off."

"Same here. It's a glitch."

"I know."

"So?"

"What should I do?"

"Anything going through when it went off?"

"It was Ted. Ted Koontz? I let him through."

"Monitor's been broke for months. It's nothing."

"How do I turn it off? Won't it alert the Border Patrol Station?"

"Shit. I'll have to authorize it from where you are. That's the only place you can turn it off. I'll be right over. Don't touch a thing. What was Ted carrying?"

"I don't know."

"Don't you have his manifest?"

"Yeah."

"What does it say?"

"Cargo."

If I burp, I will pop — no, I can't. It's too late for that. It's not even Wednesday night any more. It's Thursday morning, real early, and all I can think to say to Hector is, "Was I screaming as much as I think I was?"

"Back there? Yeah. So? Ted, we were in the pickle juice back there, real juicy, and you got us out. So, yeah, you did real good. We been sauntering down these dirt roads for hours, you know 'em like the back of your hand, so here we go. We end up back at Greenbrush Draw. No one's gonna look for us here. You okay now?"

"I gotta take off my underwear."

"Go for it."

I open my door, the light goes on inside the truck. Hector is all lit up. He squints in the sudden light, so he looks like he's being strangled. I turn to step out, stop, go, "What do you think it is?"

Hector shakes his head.

"Well, it's not a bomb, right? It's not a bomb. Can't be."

"I don't think it's a bomb."

I get out of the truck, leave the door open so I can see a little. Star light. Moon light. So back in to the scraggly brush to leave my filth. Use tissue to clean up.

I yell out, "We are so fucked!"

A hoot answers. Fuck nature.

I'm cold. Finish. Gag. Hold it. This ain't no dream.

Hector calls out, "How many people know about your place in the warehouses?"

I haven't had a party in eons. If having two or three guys over for beers and microwaved dinners counts as a party. "Hardly anybody," I answer. I walk up to the truck. "Pass me that water, gotta rinse my hands."

Hector tosses me the water bottle.

I pour a handful in to a cupped palm, scrub my hands together. Instantly, they are frozen. My guts turn somersaults.

Hector says, "Well, we can't stay here forever. But it's not safe to go back to your place. It'll be coming on dawn before you know it."

I can't think what to say, how to answer, so go, "Thursday." Then scrub my hands against my pants to dry them.

"We can't stay here."

"No helicopters."

"Not yet."

"What do you think it is?"

"It's heavy. Took them four guys to get it in our truck."

"I knew something wasn't — I could feel it."

"Stop. Too late for that now."

He looks so serious. The light in the cab opens a window in to him I don't want to see.

I climb back in, saying, "We can hide in the desert. They'll never find us. Or we dump it and get outta here. We head for Deming. Beautiful downtown Deming! I like New Mexico."

"I don't know."

I pull the door shut, the light goes off. It was getting aggravating anyway, making me worry at the sight of his face. Now I gotta say something again. I settle on, "What do you mean?"

"I can't figure what happened. Who was shooting who. What happened back there, Ted? Who were those people?"

"They weren't the people from Mexico."

"I know that. Why — how did it go down that way?"

"Maybe somebody got killed."

"Can you check your phone?"

"I'm afraid to turn it on."

"No way of knowing."

"We'll find a little abandoned rancho out in the desert. Take water, supplies, until it blows over."

I see Ted's madness ripple through his folds in shiny contrails, until he doesn't know what he's saying. His meat bag is his puppet, and he's hiding behind his eyes, manipulating body parts. He is so hesitant, tip toeing through his presence. He's sure reality will tumble. At any second, he could bolt and run. Scramble to safety. But he's gotta work, bring in the do-re-mi. He tries hard. He wants it the way he wants it.

Hiding out in the desert with him would work, if we wanted to kill each other. The blast zone is not a place to survive in. It's a place to pass through. There's no desert any more. Maybe back in the day, the desert offered favors to those who knew how to find them. There was water. Still, it's good to be afraid of the blast zone. He won't try seriously to hide out. He's got one priority: his truck. He's connected to his truck. He goes where it goes.

Maybe I should dump him? Get lost. Nobody saw me, nobody can identify me. This moment's like a seizure, its sites, its glories, its fails. I gotta see where it goes. No, I don't. I do. Border zone nightmare in pink. They always shoot the Mexican first. We can't be driving around forever.

Brush plus dark equal shapes. Ted plus me equal shitstorm. Load plus guns equal death.

Sticking out of the brush, I barely make out a century plant stalk, zig zagging high, in a symmetry, like a symbol, like a letter from a foreign alphabet. What does it say?

lone winter shaft

I go, "Well, we can't stay here."

Hector says, "What did you see? Let's go over it."

"I don't know...why?"

"Come on, it could be a help later."

"Like get our stories straight?"

"Something like that."

"All I know is we did our pick up, got through the border, no trouble. I pull in to the dollar store, park up front, leave the truck running."

"So you could go in and get Mr. Dollar."

"Right. I leave the truck on, nobody in the parking lot, and go on in. There's a cashier, a young guy, upfront. There's a hippy in the back, going down an aisle. Like one of those old hippies from Coltrane."

"You know him?"

I shake my head. "I tell the cashier to let him know I'm here."

Mya doesn't like my name Crow but I don't care. Her generation is full of phonies so they're hyper-sensitive about phoniness. The epitome of phoniness is the dollar store, which is why I'm here. Phony food. Phony goods. O, how the intelligentsia of Coltrane would cringe! High school is the paradigm — positioning is all...even when all is null. Except for Mya. Mya is learning me to be a friend, and a good neighbor. She is not a daughter-like figure. I could never paternalize her spitfire. I didn't get her anything for Christmas. Wonder if she got any presents. I'll pick up something for her here. A candied teddy bear? A chemistry set? But suppose one of the gente from Coltrane, my old crowd, see me in here. I remember how that Coltrane shaman got caught wolfing down Coney dogs behind the gas station, the gas station's Coney dogs notorious for pink slime filler in a bouquet of molecular madness. Ever after, he was known as the Coney Shaman, until he got impaled on the full rack of a bull elk, going superfast on his motorcycle. So what should it be? Energy bars! Pure sugar and fat and chemicals. The perfect gift. In German 'gift' means poison. I'm supposed to be eating natural and organic. It's impossible. Where can I get organic cilantro, today, to leach the metals from my body burden? Body burden is so Shakespearean. 'Whose body burden bakes my bodkin?' It doesn't matter because it's too late. We're bags of plastics and metals now. Giant molecules bivouacking in our home turf. We're waiting for the implosion. The device of our stasis is what our bods keep to suffice. Kant said 'sufficient' on his death bed. We're going to the same place. Might as well. If Mya knew I imbibed this filthy stuff, she'd be so upset with me.

How will I get home tonight? I can walk. Not that far. Maybe the portly gent with the truck who just came in can give me a lift. Now, another man, an older dood, in nice clothes, comes out of the back, walks over like he owns the place. He stands opposite the trucker. The trucker guy gives him a little wave, points out to the truck. His movements and his demeanor — he acts like a kid. Then he heads out the front door of the store. The older man has a stiff face, but he follows him out.

What should I get? What should I get? Better be fast, if I want to ask for a ride. Up and down the aisles, a couple things in my basket already — prunes and pop tarts. The cashier is giving me the eye.

There's a pop.

Pop?

Another!

Loud!

Glass shatters!

It goes down too far in my ears, it's going in too deep into my head. Pop, pop, pop! When will it stop? Make it stop! I'm raped by the sound. Out front, more pops! Explosions! They're like mini-explosions. A cascade of small explosions and I'm petrified. The cashier has hit the dirt, prone on the floor with arms over head.

I drop the basket and stuff my pockets with whatever is handy, then jam my clothes with as much as I can: petrified ramen, honey buns from the Coolidge administration, trail mix that guarantees mouse turd reclamation, Vienna sausages of mystery meat offal. I don't know why I'm so cool, calm as a clam. I guess nothing surprises any more.

The shooting has stopped, or paused. I head for the back exit. It's got an alarm. Probably, it's broken. I push open the door. No! The alarm goes off, and I hustle out into the back parking lot, no one around, no cars parked out here, skirt it fast, into the brush and rocks and sand and broken dolls.

Disappeared.

Hector says, "You come out of the dollar store. I'm sitting in the truck. Mr. Dollar comes out. You open the truck to get in, telling Mr. Dollar you'll swing around to the back to unload."

"I remember I said 'swing'."

"Mr. Dollar says, 'everything go okay.' That's when the little white truck pulls in."

"We were all checking it out. Then it backs around fast — real fast, with its rear end to our rear end."

"Two guys in the back of the truck, two guys in front."

"They jump out. The driver, the boss, you could tell right away."

Hector sits back. He's shaking his head, I think.

Then he must be sighing. I can hear that. He must have his eyes closed. I can't tell. Then he says, "I can picture it. I was at a weird angle, kinda hard to see."

All I can picture is dirty underwear. But I see what he's doing. I say, "Mr. Dollar starts walking to the little white truck, goes, 'what's going on'."

"How the hell would we know. Pickup and delivery — that's all we know. The driver of the little white truck walks around his truck, I remember that, him coming towards Dollar and you."

I'm trying to remember, trying not to burp with my butt. "What does he say? What does he say?"

"I couldn't hear very good, but something like, 'we'll take it now'."

"Right. Right." I close my eyes. It happened so fast. The guy goes 'we'll take it now'. "And Mr. Dollar goes, 'you will not. There were arrangements, guarantees. I don't know you.' He starts walking backwards to me, real slow like."

"That's when the driver pulls out his gun, and he takes a step back."

"Must have been stuck in the back of his pants."

"And Mr. Dollar pulls out a gun. Big freaking pistol."

"I don't know where he had it."

"That's when the bullets started flying. The other guys in the little truck were shooting. I think."

"I don't know. I don't know. I remember they were

all ducked down behind their truck, and Mr. Dollar got behind our truck's door."

"I don't know how many were shooting. Seems like a lot of bullets flying."

"I got back in the truck. It was still running."

"Mr. Dollar must have had backup. Maybe somebody on the roof? With a rifle? Pistol don't make sense. Hard enough to hit a target close up with a pistol. Maybe he had a shooter at the side of the store, peeking out."

"Whole lot of pistols. I got the truck in gear and swung around that little truck and away. Hi-ho Silver, away!"

"You done good."

"All those bullets flying."

"You started screaming once we were away."

"We don't have to mention that ever again."

"You're right. You got us out of there."

"Right."

"Now what?"

"It'd be a miracle if no one got hit."

"If they were, they'd have to call 9-1-1, and you know how expensive that is."

"If nobody was killed, they wouldn't call anybody."

"Probably. You have to call Mr. Dollar."

"I do?"

"You have to."

"Explain."

Hector says, "We gotta get rid of this load. And get paid. We don't know what it is. We don't know what's going on. Were those guys new players who wanted to hijack our load? Or did the pick up crew get jumpy? See what I mean? How many people are out there who would just as soon put a bullet in our heads than hear our story? We don't know nothing."

"So?"

"Wonder if the truck got hit."

"Did the truck get hit? I didn't even check."

"Without a flashlight, it'll be hard to tell."

I open the door. "I'll leave it open."

"Check it out." He points to the door. I don't wanna — I look.

Two holes in the door. Then we both walk around the truck looking for holes or leaks.

"Go ahead. Call."

I take the phone out of my jacket, thumb it, find his number, push it. He picks up right away, the first ring.

He goes, "You got it?"

"Right."

"You guys okay?"

"Yeah. You?"

"We're good. It's not been damaged or anything?"

"Right."

"You're safe? Don't tell me where you are."

"We're okay."

"Okay, so word's out. And it's crazy. Don't listen to anything you hear. This is how this is going to go down. There's too much attention right now. We'll wait a day at least. Can't wait too long. You guys lay low for twenty-four hours. Then call me back and we'll set up the delivery. Keep out of sight. Don't talk to anyone."

"What is it?"

"Less you know, the better. Call me in twenty-four hours."

"I will." I hang up, return the phone to my jacket pocket.

We get back in the truck.

Hector says, "We're gonna wear down the battery. I'm cold. Always colder before the dawn."

"We can't stay here. Delivery in twenty-four hours."

I stare through the dark at Ted's face. Where it should be.

Where are the space people, I wonder. That'll come down in a flash and make all the action figures' parts reassemble in the proper way? Reborn, then, heroes and bads can get back to the work they were meant for, playing their simple version of good and evil. Because this version, this vast vacant stare at dawn in the blast zone, means we mess up, we're dead. I wonder if they have dollar stores in heaven.

Chapter Nine

If we lived on Chitin Planet, everybody would be armored. Or enamored. Plus, you can digest chitin. Thus, we end up living on bugs. I don't think Mona will eat bugs. Ever. Even if she was starving. She believes in simplicity because her parents are so meager with excess. Egrets. Regrets. Waddles. Great fit wadi. Wie gehts? Ça va? Wassup? Where ya' going? Herculaneum. Hibernaculum. Years in bears. Why don't they rhyme? But years in beers do? (Mona will never talk to me again.) The Painter will show up in Saginaw. The world will go pink, and everybody will sink, sink, sink, in the pink, pink, pink. I'm telling our fortune!

This mood moody mood moods me to moods.

Got back from our run a while ago, started to undress to clean up, settled on time travel all afternoon. Sinks are useless without water. Our water line is off. Or you get a nasty muddy slew from the faucet. Dad's assigned to the treatment plant until further notice. Mom left early with her riot gear and not for the prison's New

Year's masquerade. There are no toys. There's no fun. Everything is tainted with utmost corruption. Mona's never seen a giant ground sloth. Neither have Mom and Dad. They must become windows and see what's there. Mountains go up. Blue is a room. Secret messages are spied and overheard. Inside is a nest where I don't have to look. I need water. I need Mona. I almost think 'I need pink' but think better of it, so insert it sideways. From here on, everything will be in 3-D Technicolor. Maybe Crow has water. But if I go outside, I'll scream. I won't. I haven't turned on my phone. I'm sick of my notochord overflowing with trivial pursuit. I don't feel like the funniest person in the world.

I don't bother with shoes or socks, so get over to Crow's front door on tip toe, braving the sand and rocks and stingers. No bites. Am I in the right place? I was out the front door faster than light, then forgot my promise to scream, because outside's molasses engulfed. How did I get over so fast? (I bolted!) Gray, gray...deep gray...cloudbanks across my mountains. The houses are gray around here, sinking into torpor, but Crow's is vibrating. No rain yet. What is rain? What's molasses? What's sorghum?

Syrups, an all out word.

Crow opens the door, says, "Are you coming in, or admiring the view?"

I put on my space helmet and enter the dodo underground underwater.

"Look at your dirty feet!"

"Do you have a bidet?"

"A bidet is not for your feet."

"Do you have water?"

"Drinking or bathing?"

"We can't even flush the toilet."

"They say it could be twenty-four hours. But we're on a different line or something. Well, come in. I've got treats, presents. *Sorpresa.*"

"What's the occasion?"

"It's New Year's. Plus, I didn't get you anything for Christmas."

I go Neanderthal and grunt. Crow's in a robe. Maybe he just got out of the shower. He must have plenty of water. I follow him in to the kitchen. I see the leg braces, or whatever you call them, hanging from the beam on the ceiling. The place has the same light as outside, though a little bit warmer than outside. The oven's on, the door's open. The source! Crow's in his shelves, riffling bags and boxes.

"Here," he says, "chickies," and he hands me a yellow cardboard box of yellow peeps.

"Wow," I say, "these must be from last Easter."

"Oh, they don't decay."

"Thanks.
"You're in a mood. PMS?"

"Mood? How's your PMS? You seem pretty up actually."

"These last couple days have been extraordinary. I know you felt it, too. Since I saw you last — when was that?"

"Couple days ago."

"I can tell you want to say something first. You want tea? I'll make us tea. You go first, then I'll tell my story."

"Track team? Four of us took a run down Greenbrush Draw this morning. Mona came, but she didn't run. Mona isn't talking to me now — "

"But that's another story. Go on." He gets the kettle on the burner, turns the burner on. Three cups laid out.

"We found the pink. The place where it was spilled."

"Didn't you run there the other day?'

"Yeah. Yeah. So, we're looking at this gross, viscous, pink mess — "

"And the Painter showed up?"

"No! The law. Some guy in regular clothes and a guy in a suit. Had to be a fed."

"They take your names?"

"No. They knew we didn't do it."

"They were staking out the place, thinking they'd catch the Painter."

"Maybe. But, you know, with what happened last night at the dollar place, then they show up?" Elaborate roll of my shoulders.

He looks ethereal. But only for a few seconds. "Co-ink-a-dink?" he warbles out the question mark. He gulps. "Are you going to the party tomorrow?"

"Does everybody know about it?"

"You mean, even old people? Artists in Coltrane see it as a happening. All sorts of shenanigans are planned. All over the place. Partying like it's 1968."

"Wow. Sigh. Sigh." Everything is gray in this house. Light some candles, dood! Does a house make a home? Around here, houses are not always homes, neither are they places. When humans leave, a house doesn't go back to nature. A house goes post-human — place becomes empathy wreckage. Home in the blast zone!

"Things're moving fast, Mya. Immediately, we want it to stop. But, maybe, sometimes things are so up, there's no other way. It feels physical. Light comes, goes. We don't get a lot of days like this. Maybe it'll rain."

"Maybe it'll snow."

"Take care, Mya." He's staring at me deep. More overlap, not telepathy, like Mona says. But I'm registering his concern. He says, "Mya! Mya, whatever's going on, you're ready. Up to now's been boot camp. You're full of care. You don't have to take anything. I'd say you are careful and carefree, which sounds like a paradox."

"Like me."

"Exactly. Coltish and whimsical. Well, not so much today maybe. What did you do to your throat? Vampire?"

I ignore that. "'Coltish'? I'll have to remember that for Mona." Then a pause for emphasis and: "What about careless? Sounds like you can't be careless with careless."

"Exactly."

"What's your story, morning glory? Tell!"

"Mine's a two-parter. First, last night, Wednesday night, I was at the dollar store when the gun fight broke out."

"No!"

"Yes! It was insane. I know, I know. Beyond surreal to total death match 2000."

"What did you do?"

"I snuck out the back door."

"Did you have to talk to the cops?"

"No way. I headed home fast as I could."

"You could have been shot. O, God! You're okay? What happened?" I move towards him barely, like maybe to go in for a hug or at least a touch, but he holds up his hand 'stop'.

Crow shakes all over — a shiver, and gets up to check the water, not quite at a boil. He leaves the sad or startled or frightened face, and he takes on a simple gray and white, gray and white demeanor.

I pry, "Part Dieux?"

He lowers his voice: "An old friend showed up who I haven't seen in a long time. He has throat cancer, so he's come to say goodbye."

I'm barely coping with all this information, when the bathroom door, on the other side of the house from where we are, opens. We turn to look. It's Tiresias! Naked. (Schlong.)

He rasps, "Oh, sorry. Didn't know we had company. I

heard voices but I'm so used to Matthew talking to himself." He shrugs. "Do you have another robe?"

Octopus whippersnapper! There's a loosed tentacle uncovered —

Crow calls out, "Behind the bathroom door, behind the bathroom door!"

He goes to fetch it.

"Matthew?"

"Don't."

"We met earlier."

Crow says, "I know. I want Ty to enjoy figuring it out on his own."

"Ty?"

"Short for Tyrell. Tyrell Mobley of the Charleston Mobley's."

"No way."

"Way."

Ty comes out of the bathroom with a robe on. He looks different, the same. Fluffy robe. He walks over, smiling to me. "Matthew, this is the girl I was telling you about who was so funny. In the arroyo?" He notices me noticing the surprise of it.

We try so hard to keep our cool, even when we're really surprised.

I say, "We met in Greenbrush Draw."

"By the pink. Mya and Mona. I remember your names— "

"Because you were peeking! Spying on us."

"No bad. No bad. Not for any bad reason. We overlapped. I was walking in. You were running in. Pink in the middle. Grotesque."

"Easy, brother," says Crow. "Have tea with us? Come. We'll sit at the table and talk of the death of kings."

We sit around the table with our tea. I put my peeps on the table. The yellow stands out, belonging oddly, because inside, here, now, makes a nest. Outside, a dream. Yellow seems to speak, to say out loud, 'Yellow!'

Finally, I say, "You have water."

Crow slurps at his tea, says, "Don't ask me. I don't understand it. Take what you want. I have jugs. You can go home and get your containers. Fill 'em up."

I nod. "Can I take a shower?"

"Of course. Clean your feet, girl!"

Ty, or Tiresias, pushes back in his chair, glances under the table. "Wow. Dirty feet." He gets up and goes in to the kitchen area, finds a stray plastic wash tub and fills it with leftover hot water. He adds cold. Gets it just right. He whips some dish soap in to the tub of water with his hand, then carries it over to me. He puts it down by me. Taps my knee so I know to swing out. He kneels, reaches for a foot. He holds my left foot carefully, with both hands, like he's handling a baby kitty. He gently guides my foot around to the tub. He lowers it, so my toes are touching, and with his other hand he pushes up my sweat pants leg, then immerses my dirty foot in the tub. Then he does the same with my right foot. He says in a small voice, "Soak. I'll get a towel."

The warm water is stirring. My space helmet crackles, pops. I disintegrate. Their hominess gets in. I guess gray doesn't matter. Taking care of each other does. I'm not underwater, just my feet.

Crow's watching the whole thing. A slack smile, a bit of a droop to it.

Ty returns with a towel and wash cloth, goes to his knees before me. He reaches in for a foot, takes my left, and holds it over the water. He scrubs at my foot with the wet wash cloth, over the top and toes then the sole. It's electric through my body. No one's ever handled my feet. I didn't even know they were connected like that.

I'm so embarrassed that Crow can read it in my face, and he says, "Go with it. You're good. And don't think the chickies were your *sorpresa*. That was a joke."

I manage, "That feels fine. Thanks."

"Tell us what happened with Mona," says Crow.

Slowly, I try to talk — try not to tickle. His fingers and the wash cloth probe between my toes, rubbing each toe.

(I'm a duck-billed platypus. This has gotta be good for the flippers.)

The feeling of warm, soapy water, caressed feet, worked over, is galactic. I feel so clean.

I try again to talk. I will look at my feet. It comes out in chirps like I'm a sudden bird: "Mona made this shrine to Tonantzin. After our run this morning, she wanted us to hitch down to her place. To see the shrine. So we could drip a few drops of our blood on it."

"Who's Tonantzin?" asks Crow.

Ty says, "She's all over Mexico. You see shrines to her all the time. Like the mother goddess."

"Changing Woman. This is her place. Our place."

Crow says, "She wants to be blood sisters."

"I know, just a pin prick. But it wasn't the blood that bothered me. It's the hassle! Hitching down to Naco, then hitching back later by myself."

Ty says, "It's dangerous?"

Crow snorts. "No, kemosabe, there's no traffic."

"It can take hours and it's less than ten miles. Mona thinks I'm chicken. That's what she said. Afraid to stick myself. She got mad. Like she was insulted."

My feet are naked as they've ever been. My toes and feets want to grab! I ain't no bird, not like a bird at all. For reals, pure human synergy. Predatory feets are living things attached to my stems.

Crow says, "Sillies! She won't stay mad. She knows you're no chicken."

Ty lets me soak. With a rasp, he says, "When I was a little kid, my ma used to tell us boys, 'if kids start teasing you, calling you chicken, just look 'em in the eye and say, yes, I am.'"

"I feel like I'm melting."

"You're done," says Ty. "Here, here's the towel. Dry your feet."

I lift my feet from the water, place them on the towel he's set next to it.

Crow gets up from the table, heads for the kitchen. He comes back and plops a bag of trail mix in my lap. "Merry Christmas, Mya-bug."

I warble, "And peeps! Your largesse has no bounds."

Ty says, "I don't think it was hitching or pricking your finger that kept you from Mona's shrine. I don't think so — "

Chapter Ten

If I say I have to go to the bathroom, I can leave the kids in the living room, and cut through the kitchen on the way, so I can real easy swing open the fridge door and stick my finger right in to the pico for a finger full. I need one more bite. Good stuff. I'm starving. Then after I come out of the bathroom, I can rejoin the kids, then say I gotta get some more soda, so slide back out to the kitchen to snatch one of those leftover pork chops I saw back there in the fridge. Last night's supper? Plus, of course, a smart water. I can stick the chop in my pocket or gulp it down there. Hector and Cecilia are talking in her bedroom. That's great. No one will know. I come back out to the kids, them's so busy with Tetris, I munch my chop. Two bites. I'm so hungry, I could eat a horse. I feel weak from hunger, sludging here on Hector's friend's couch, behind kids stretched out on the floor before the flatscreen. The night out in the desert was cold and hungry. Now it's Thursday, and I need to keep up my strength. Maybe Cecilia can make burritos out of the leftover pork chops. Her breakfast burrito an hour ago was chorizo and egg. Real good. I needed three more.

Cecilia and Hector come out of the back. I can hear the door open, then I can hear their voices. Hector's saying, "I wouldn't do anything that would endanger you or the kids."

She goes, "That's what men always say. Don't write that story here, Chico!"

"What story?"

"You don't even know what it is. It's gotta be some nasty shit."

"Not so loud."

She huskily whispers, "For a few hours?"

Hector says — and now they've walked into the kitchen: "Yeh. Till the sun goes down. We need to catch a few hours of sleep. The truck's three blocks over, behind that empty building with the wall overgrown with brush. It's not invisible but if anybody interested finds it, they'll have no way of connecting it to here. See what I mean? We'll be out of here soon as we can."

It's my turn to say something, because all I can think of is pork chops. I call out, "Don't make it sound so mysterious. No big deal. We're not criminals."

She answers, "'Mysterious', he says, when the neighbors saw a pink coyote last night. And last night, too, there was that shootout." She's moving in to the living room, right up towards me. She glances at the kids playing Tetris. Girls are so good at Tetris. Or is that an urban myth? I guess she doesn't care if the kids hear: "If the feds connect you to that, you realize how many law enforcement agencies will be looking for you?"

I say, "Cecilia, thanks for the breakfast burrito.

Usually I only have Mexican food on Tuesdays."

Cecilia laughs. The girl looks up right away at her mom. So sharp, that girl is all eyes and a good gamer. Cecilia says, "Know what they call Mexican food in Mexico?"

I respond, "I've been down there. I'm not some dumb ass who hasn't been around."

She turns to Hector, who's behind her, but to the side, looking distracted. I get it. He's embarrassed, because he had to tell this woman what's going on. But it's not drugs! Breakfast burrito. Tetris. Nap. I call Mr. Dollar as we agreed. We set it up, time and place. We're out of here. Me and Hector need to figure where to meet. A safe place. What's a good place? That we know. Where should we meet for the drop, the pass off, the giveaway, the delivery, getting the deed done, over and out? Want this done so bad! One more step. Don't get caught. I bet the kids have candy stashes hidden in their rooms. Is there any way I can make up a story that would put me in their rooms? Nothing creepy. Cecilia's basically gearing up to yell at me. Where should I sit? Should I move? Should I go? I should stand up. I don't belong here. I have to stay here. Keep low. Me and Hector figured it out overnight on those rough roads that go nowhere in the desert. We have a call to make.

She says to Hector, "This your boss?"

"He's okay," says Hector.

"He thinks I'm Mexican. Kids, what are we?"

The little girl and little boy go cute as you please: "God's angels!"

The girl, who's bigger and older, gets up from the floor. She's looking at me. She says, "Want to play? I bet you're good."

"I am good," I say.

She says, "You're a friend of Hector's?"

"I guess so."

"X-Man, scoot over, let him play."

The little boy protests. Big sister explains, "He can't really play but he thinks he can."

This is one heavy chick.

The boy gives his control to me and melts away to his mom. He grabs her around the waist and butt. He starts hugging and laughing at the same time. Mom's laughing too. Everybody's smiling except Hector, still standing off to the side looking distracted.

The girl says, "Go!"

We begin. She's fast. Faster than me. But I know the patterns. 'Use the force!' Settle in to slaughter —

It goes so fast. The other kid has unwrapped from his mother. He points to me and says, "Mommy, he stinks." She swats his butt. He stomps off. The mother walks over to Hector.

Before the girl can hit it again, I say, "Wait! Timeout, timeout! I forgot, what're your names again? I like to know the names of those I am about to conquer."

The girl chortles, back on her stomach, stretched out, but she turns to me and smiles. "Kaylen."

"And the boy child?"

"Xavier with an X."

"Nice."

"Ready."

"Prepare to die."

Mom is like one of those Jeopardy moms but I'm focused so can't, won't, don't —

But the girl hasn't engaged. She's still looking at me. She says, "What's your favorite book?"

"I don't know."

"Wrong answer. I know Hector's."

"I have too many."

"Name one."

"*Lord of the Rings.*"

"Good answer."

"What's your favorite?"

"*Charlotte's Web.*"

"I saw the movie. Spider girl? What's Hector's? Hey, hey! Hey, you didn't say, 'go!' I wasn't ready."

She laughs like a demon, jolting into the game. "LOTR is actually three books."

I yell, "You didn't ask my name."

"I remember."

"Do not."

She goes, "T-E-D."

Chapter Eleven

10:00 PM — a good time!

Party time!

It's cold and wet. I dressed in layers. My hair is crazy wild fun under my hoodie. It's all about layers. It's all in the timing, when to get to a party. I've been to two parties. That's not counting blast zone rendezvous when a bunch of kids hang out in the desert smoking weed. No, three, if you count Mouse's bar b q. Mouse buried a couple javelina in his backyard in hot coals, stuffed with chiles and onions and corn and potatoes. The carcasses looked like dogs. My dad said it tasted like pork. They'd burned two little witch dogs in the sand, burnt them right up to crispy critters. We got there early, stayed late. Mom drove home.

My first party was Elsa Gonzalez' seventh birthday party. She was petrified with xenophobia. I barely knew the girl. Her mom and my mom knew each other. Elsa's mom had scrounged up some real live birthday cake candles. When she lit them and carried in the flaming cake, kids cried. Was it too gorgeous? My second party was a Training/Testing Social when I was thirteen. Mona and I went. They played tunes, served classic Coke. We ate plantain chips and sweet potato dip. Kids danced. Mona danced with Tommy Winter, the cutest boy in that age bracket. They made out. Her first time. I went home by myself.

Druggies say, 'it's all in the timing'. You got to time your drugs, make them work, make them last. Then the druggies like to say, 'a five dollar hamburger can ruin a fifty dollar high'.

Cecil's house is dark, wearing shadows like drapes or capes. Maybe the front window has a glow from maybe a single bulb, maybe off to the side, or maybe in the back. A scant, scary glow, but I ain't afraid of no ghosts. We're practically neighbors. Got over here in black splat step. Wet! I was thinking of parties. The car's here. No hesitation, I go to the front door and knock. The window fronts a dim aquarium. I will not look for nudibranchs, cuttlefish, or electric gobies. They're in bed.

Cecil's mom opens the door. She's wearing a skin suit, skinny little thing, with sad eyes. I woke her. Or else she hasn't chilled in a thousand years.

"I'm sorry," I say. "I hope I didn't wake you up. I was looking for Cecil."

"He's not here."

"Oh. Okay."

"That boy! Gotta sick little sister, and he's out all hours after those scorpions. Turns out, you milk 'em, you get top dollar for their jizz."

"That's great," I say.

"Poor little girl's been sick all week. Since Christmas. Can't afford to take her to the doctor. But that boy's out trying to get some cash on a night like this."

"I hope she feels better. You take care. Happy New Year's."

"I *take* what I can. Yeah. Happy new year."

It's, what, five miles to Saginaw?

Fix my jacket, my hoodie, hurry out to the highway, stop, pirouette, start walking, heading east. Stop. Look around. Only a couple street lights work. Tall, praying mantis types. I stare at them, trying to make them go on. Depends on my fling. The lit ones cast an egg wash in a bullet shape down from their bulbs, with a corona of gray around that, like a dim halo.

Hitch? Stand and wait?

Hike it?

Go home.

The evening was moist.

Lights in the west. They're white circles the size of life savers. They tease the black around them blue. They must be coming from my 'hood. I probably know them. They'll give me a ride. Should I get out my flashlight and wave them down?

Too late, too late. Too late to get in to my pack and retrieve the flashlight.

It's a pickup. Blue at one time. A little pickup.

Three guys crammed up front, two in the back. I got my thumb out. They stop. All three in the front are wearing pink shirts or pink jackets. Same for the guys in back. The guy on the passenger side lowers his window. I recognize him. He recognizes me, smiles. The boys are ogling me. Their eyes are liquid.

The boy says, "Going to the party?"

"Of course," I offer.

"Show us some pink."

I open my jacket to show the pink sweatshirt I'm wearing. Layers.

"Hop in."

Five boys, fairly human. I hop in. I nod to the guys in back. They have fun eyes, too. Whew! Doods be lit already! Get comfortable, back pressed to the side. We lurch forward. Right away, the wind comes on deadly, buffeting us. We hunker in like turtles.

Dirty boys. I recognize three of them, two up front, one back here. But I don't know them. I guess they're from here. I've seen them around. I might have had them in classes back in the day, but I can't be sure. Because now they're a bit vacant, tripping balls, stoned out of their gourds, and it's New Year's Eve and the biggest party of all time.

Did I bring pepper spray?

No way. No bad vibes. Keep it: kids from here, we're all from the same kibbutz. We've met. People. It's natural. Going to the party.

Now I'm getting wet. In Coltrane we never turn

away from water. I'll dry out. We barge along fast and certain. We know where we're going. Pretty soon (duck billed platypus is replaced by Thylacine!), we turn off the highway to the road in to Saginaw. There's the old cemetery.

The driver has to slow down right away because the road's so bad. Not just pot holes, these are great and giant continents of Pangaea breaking up with chasms between them. The truck lights make the narrow torture track sparkle. It's lined with drippy trees, pines, oaks. All a-sparkle. We're talking party time! A whoop builds in my throat. Up ahead, lights, a clot of them, a vortex penetrating, pushing back the black and white. The boys in the back with me give out hoots. Mine's a whoop.

We hear music. A deep steady beat. Cars and pickups, a few vans, parked every which way along the road, so that continuing on is sketchy, squeezing through bumpers or headlights sticking out too much. People are walking along the road. Pink jackets. Pink hats. Pink scarves. Dirty fading, gray pink away from light. Oh, I see! Light triggers pink. The nebula hive of flickering lights marks *Party House.* We're almost there. We go down a sparkle tunnel to a glow stick party filled with lightning bugs. The guy near me hangs over the side, shouting to the driver, "Park! Park anywhere. Park!"

We creep along. People shout to us. I don't know the words. Our boys shout back, but not in any regular Babel. It's disorder by public demand — contraband. The passenger side door opens and discharges two doods in pink shirts. The guy who was in the middle falls to the ground, rolls to his feet, slapping at his clothes to knock off the gunky. No biggie tonight. It's clean filth tonight.

Ready to roll. The guys in the back jump out,

leaving me after all we've been through. The truck's barely moving. But no parking: the driver'll have to keep going, park down a ways. I figure it's time. Here's the house — big wooden monstrosity, two story job, but the top seems to have collapsed in places. I jump.

What we got here is a ton of peeps milling about in/on yard, porch, house. People hustle in and out of the front door of the battered old house: sibyls, dryads, leprechauns, trolls, goddesses, young and old, of all fallen kingdoms, dressed in pink finery, pink now aglow. Giddy cluster. Music comes from inside where a solar charged boombox demands ears. Techno electronics throb bass, like a grenade lobbed in there, exploding in slow motion. Lots of people have glow sticks and flashlights. Battery powered lanterns hang at strategic spots, by the front door, on the porch. No electricity. I walk in to the yard, crossover. Screeches, screams, shouts, giggles. Couples making out. Threesomes doing whatever. Everyone seems to have a red plastic cup. Where's the beer? Doods pile up wood, branches, chairs, into a pyramid, in the middle of the scraggly front yard. I can't keep from slithering. I got to get inside, grab a brew, scope it out. I recognize people. It's a small town. I'm the official wallflower of the biggest party of all time.

Make my move. Smiles, snorts, stinks! "Hi, there!" "Snap! I know you." A guy in pink pants goes, "Look at all the pregnant virgins." "Fuck it! Get blazed!" Easy as a snake, I'm past the incipient bonfire, up the steps to the wraparound porch. Lots of the old places had wrap around porches. Ma and Pa set out of a summer evening, hoping for a microscopic breeze, watching UFOs up top, through the trees, in the zoo of outer space. Mona wouldn't like zoo. The porch is made of gray boards which don't seem related to trees any more. Skeletal casts. Too many people on the porch, too many dancing. We're afloat, adrift, at sea on the deck of a galleon teeming with happy penguins. My giddies turn to tremblies. Get off the porch! Right now. Push through. "Hi there, lady!" "Party!" Then: "Painter party!" At the door, a young man, about my age, goes, "Happy New Year!" The guy behind him, kinda pushing him forward out the door, while I sidle by, says, "Too early! It's not time, douche." I'm in. Thylacine ain't worried.

Blazing dancers weave together like mating birds. This is how whales do it, underwater foreplay, weightless in the green sauna. It's bigger inside than outside. People take pictures with their phone's, filming it. Flashes pop! I expand! Pounding beat. My feet move, thump. I pull down my hood, open my jacket. So close now, I'm occupied. It's in me, poking, pulling, pushing. I make for the side, away from the dance floor, where the kegs are. A giant bong is thrust in to my hands by a girl with a single, long pink dread rising from the center of her head. The bong is techy glassware with a touch of steampunk mad scientist. I take it, figure the carburetor, take a hit. Pass it on. Over to the kegs. Bunch of guys standing around the kegs. None of them in pink. None of them checks a phone, or dances. They, tough guys. Bad boys. Over ripe men battered by needs. They can't tear their eyes from their fear. They are so afraid and can't let anyone know. There's Otis! I know Otis. I pump out my beer, take a swig, leave my donation. Otis has materialized right next to me.

I shout, "Getting a beer?" I have to stand on tip toe to reach his ear. He turns on me fast, so his face grazes mine. I step back.

"Already had seven. That's my lucky number," he shouts.

"What are you guys doing?" I motion to his *compadres.*

"Ha! We're waiting for the Painter. We got a net, hand cuffs, the works."

"What are you going to do with him?"

He shuffles closer. Even through jacket and shirt, I can tell his muscles are twitching so much he's writhing, like he's got rats under his skin. "You wanna dance? You smell good."

"I just got here. I'm gonna look around." I back away slowly, smiling, keep my arms at my sides, lower my eyes — don't want to spook him.

A guy near me yells at another guy beside him, "Wanksta!" The other guy erupts, his whole body a solid piston shove into the shouter. I slide away, then around the perimeter of dancers. How do you get upstairs? Down here, walls have been knocked out, until the whole first floor is one big dance hall. In the back, what might have been the kitchen. All that's left is a double sink, now filled with girls, their butts squeezed in to the sinks, their pink wrapped legs and pink boots kicking out from the gray steel. No water! Must be uncomfortable unless your butt fit. Guys collect by the sink girls. The girls laugh way too loud and hard. I shift course. Sounds smother. A few older guys in pink robes share a joint in a corner. Walk backwards, forwards, turn in a circle. No one cares. No one listens or watches at a party. Another group, in an entrance to what might have been a pantry, have blow torch, wire, little caps that look like lip balm containers. Wire in the balm, torch it, inhale. Say the magic word. Very complicated!

Pounding beat.

My beer's warm. Makes my guts clench. Where are my bubbles? I need bubbles —

"Hey, beautiful!" I don't twitch at first, unsure who's talking to who. But, then: "Tonantzin!"

I swing around and it's Crow, also in pink robes, joining the older guys, getting in line for the doob. I smile and he smiles. I go over to him, shout, "Where's Ty?"

"Home resting."

"How'd you get here?"

"Oh, been prepping all day in Coltrane. You know it's all in the timing. Were you looking for a ride? Well, you're here now, my little tortilla chip."

"Have you seen — "

"Don't say it! Don't say her name or you'll drive her away. Let it happen."

I think I was gonna say, 'have you seen any bubbles?' I am such a liar! I am hideous, ugly, and my hair is on fire...no, my hair has cramps. Coils of crackly. Crunchy. I'm an inverse vamp munching Thylacines.

He gets busy with the joint, then hands it to me. Toke it, pass it. I wander out of the kitchen zone, back towards the kegs, where boys are pounding each other in the head with their fists. Dancers scream, pull away. Other boys break it up, toss the offenders out the front door. A great cheer goes up. Otis's in the thick of it. Self-appointed security. That's so so so —

Someone pulls at my sleeve. I turn and it's Donna Pardo with a bright pink face. She shouts, "I didn't paint myself all over, just my face, because I didn't want to asphyxiate."

I bend in, give her a little hug. There's the other praying mantis, Will. He's being shy, sipping at his red cup, managing to avoid my eyes and to stay close to Donna at the same time. What philosophy they will invent in their curiosity rodeo! I can't imagine tiny Donna climbing his beanpole.

All at once faces stand up and make demands. Faces require so much work. Nearby, familiar faces, faces I highlight with extra credit. It's uncanny! All there is is faces. Faces bobbing faces. Faces with features. Face like empties. How do I tell faces apart? It comes with the territory, like a special prize, bonus items in your existence package. Faces party, frolic, duel. Faces kiss, parley, drool. Break it up! No fighting allowed. Rapt instead. Rein it in. Sugar faces, right here, Hillary and Tremayne, with their meat bags in tow. (OMG.) What's next? Rains of blood? Talking catfish? Have to remember that for Mona. Hillary wants to talk. She whisper shouts into my ear, "Do you have any condoms?"

I shake my head. Hillary lets loose something about Testing or Tremayne, or maybe it's about her brother's jack, or her mom is for a fact.

Quentin with a girl wrapped around him, waves at me. In the thick, to see him, to meet eyes, to make contact, is like treatment — party on!

The big bad boys not in pink scramble together their own boom box and set it right on top of a keg. This ups the chagrin. Everybody who sees this knows what's going to happen. How it will go down. But some folks like embarrassment. They thrive on it. They get off on catastrophe. Most go, 'don't want no scene'. Others go, 'bring it on'.

Big country-style guitar licks blast from the keg's boom box. *Americana folklorica*! War is declared! No peace in Hogtown. Sounds of the Confederacy! Talk about a buzzkill. Dancers muster. Fists are clenched. Sphincters tighten. Screams and hoots. Sides form ranks. The dancers' music goes off. One of the bad boys turns off the boom box on the keg for some reason, maybe so they can hear each other scream. Yeah, he wants it flat out fisticuffs. Cry havoc and release the jellyfish of war!

I gotta get out of here. Not good! No, no, no. I'm pulp. Pulpy! In the jellyfish wars, we sting each other to death. I didn't bring my helmet. I'm not ready for this bathysphere. Why does it always go like this? So seldom are we in public in the blast zone. I mean, we never have to wear nice clothes. We don't have good clothes. We have tatterdemalion harlequin stillsuits, recycling our desperation. Sense-o-ware. Syth-o-ware. We get together so Raleigh...rarely. My hair begins to rise, the ends at first, they ascend. It must be static electricity. Thylacine fangs! The solar system works on static. We should name our solar system. Now the hairs on the back of my neck are standing up. Antigravity headgear, hair boners arc all!

No way this look can be good. I glance around for an escape route. Through the throng in thongs, I see her on the other side of the room. Face! A face in green glow. Alone to see. Alone for me. Mona. I said it, I thought it. Her hair is down in luxurious abandon, as though the evil step sisters had just been trounced and she hadn't finished quaffing. She's fussing at the dancers' boom box. She slips in a CD. *Let It Bleed's* unmistakable first few beats take over, and the shout that goes up rocks the old place's foundation.

All is forgiven! The beat goes on. Sphincters unclench. Everybody exhales. Amygdala on hold!

I'm dancing. I'm flying. Mona's beside me. We dance, we flail, we percolate! She comes in for the kill, wraps her arms around me. She shouts in my ear, "It was beauty that killed the beast!"

She won't let go. My arms are at my sides. They feel like paddles. Either to spank me or electrocute me. (Duckbilled platypus is back!) If I hold her back, touch her back, I'll explode. Sometimes I explode six times a day.

Her head curves in close to my neck, so I feel her breath. My toes curl. She shouts, "I brought you a band aid. I don't want to see your blood."

I shout, "What color it is."

"Blood red, flesh of my flesh," she shouts. "Come on!"

She unfolds from me, and we trip away from the dancers, cut for the door, Rolling Stones flaring out in shockwaves.

I stop her, shout into her ear: "How do gay men have sex?"

She smiles, shrugs, shouts back: "Fill comfortable holes like everyone else?" We both are goofy now. She's deep in my eyes with harpoons and scattergun. She shouts, "You're positively intergalactic tonight!"

"We all are. You saved the day."

"Let's go. I can barely hear you."

We take off. We stop, hurl in to each other, this pounding dance requires it. We dance like animals, each move exaggerates us. Sweaty now, we gape, wide-eyed, breathing like raptors. She leans in to my ear: "Did you see who was getting a brew?"

"Otis?"

"The guy in civilian clothes. From yesterday."

We make it to the door, as the music and dancing rise and pitch — the room's alive! The door looks like an enchanted portal, still it reveals the really good time — outside. A quick final scan before exiting does not spot any carpetbaggers or mercenaries, but — aha! I do the eye of the fed standing to the side of the dancers trying to blend in. No suit today, the dood is all button down, and his full power eye sight right in mine. He waves. He waves! We're out the door in a giggle. Ahoy, mates! The porch is rollicking, roiling at sea, sea serpents galore.

Mona pulls me along, saying, "Regular wreck of the Hephaestus."

"Wrong Hef! The fed dood is here. Just saw him seeing me."

Mona squeals: "The plot thickens! He's hot for you, babe. Reconnaissance. Surveillance. He's got it covered. He wants to uncover you. Just hang on. Let's get away."

"What do you mean?"

"I'm prepared for all contingencies."

"You're freaking me out. It keeps going up, up, then down, down. Everything."

"You're freaking me out. Come on." She takes my hand and we navigate the porch, its upright bodies, around and through them. Outside has promise! Touches, gropes, pats on the ass. All sorts of faces. Flow to flip out.

We're *flowing* literally, down the steps, my feet not touching. This is levitation lazy, me and Mona down the steps to the front yard.

I screech, "I lost my beer!"

"Don't worry. I got it covered." She bunches her shoulders so her pack rumbles. She's got my pink coat on.

The boys have had trouble getting the fire going, because, though it's not raining, *the evening was moist.* Now a dood clarifies analysis with a metal can of gasoline. Maybe it's kerosene. He slops it over the boards and chairs and trash, tosses a match, and whoosh! Bright yellow sprites tall as a man come to life with sparks and bluster. We hurry past.

Out on the road, it's not too bad. A guy vomits over a cancer tree. A girl squats to pee holding on to a hot rod's bumper. No traffic. Quieter for sure. In fact, quiet so loud, I know I'll only be able to whisper.

She says, "Let's go next door."

We can make out the neighbor house through the trees. Another haunted shack, smaller than the party house. Maybe in worse shape. We hunch up our shoulders, and head for the steps in front of the house. This was a neighborhood. People lived here, died here, planted trees here. The front steps sag. We collapse. We sit in the casual dark we are used to now. We can see enough.

Mona says, "This is nice. What time is it?" She rolls her shoulders until her pack comes around, then she's practically crawling inside it, rummaging. "Here," she says, pulling out a half pint of vodka.

"I don't have my phone." I take the small bottle. It's already been opened. I screw off the cap, take a snort. Blow up fast. Give it back to her. "Hey, where's my band-aid?"

She laughs. "You think I'm kidding?" She takes a gulp of vodka. "The goons suspect someone at the party to be the pink culprit. The Painter!"

"Makes sense."

"They're undercover. We lay a trap."

"Clandestine. Tonantzin. These guys are clueless."

One answer comes in the form of a great, blasting, rip pop, whether gunpowder or cherry bomb or electronic boom we will never know. Doods going psycho at the house. Like a cookie cutter to our ears, the startle leaves us chipped.

"Was that a hymen being popped?"

"Hope they don't burn down the place."

"Nah. Not tonight." She takes a swig, hands it to me. I swig.

She pushes: "What were you going to tell me?"

I breathe, push back: "Sometimes my imagination— "

"Sometimes it's a walking daydream —

"Hurtling through imagery, you know?

"And I see things. I call it Cascades."

"Cascades." She scowls. "Do the voices in your

head tell you to do terrible things?"

I humpf. "I didn't want you to worry. Get distracted."

"Who's distracted? We know the score. I know you know I know you know."

"I see things. All the time. Sometimes."

"We all do. There's so much to see every second. My little peanut butter cup is so sensitive, like a delicate flower."

"I'll delicate you!" I scoot in to attack —

A sound behind us makes us jump. We whip around and what we imagined might be the start of a cave-in turns out to be a white cat making an entrance. Ah, the front door is hanging on by a thread and kitty curdling by it made it creak.

"Do you see that?"

I nod. "Kitty, kitty."

The cat meows, pads over to us, stops, drops, gets comfortable, stretching out by us.

"He likes us," says Mona.

"How do you know it's a he?"

"Ask him."

"Are you a he?"

The cat has pretty much assumed the cat lounging position but keeps his head up, ghosty white face with flashy eyes. The cat says, "Vichyvichyvichy."

"I don't understand," says Mona.

I do. Right away. I have been getting these messages from the universe. They seem to sense make or I am blotto. I have to elaborate, tell Mona everything. But I say, "Caterwauling, right? What kitties do."

"Overlap? Talk to the animals? What does 'vichy' mean?"

"If you touch him, you'll disappear?"

'Vichyvichy' goes on and on in a helix. Cat's on a roll. Kitty with a lot on his mind. Mona wears funny puzzle face watching me. She doesn't know this code but she knows me, and this makes me feel better right away. 'Vichyvichy' makes images, parading through my head. A gang of dogs and cats in Naco, called the Curs, are massing for a surprise attack tonight on the Saginaw Runaways. But the bonfire is a perfect intervention. Cease fire! Everyone maintains his or her dignity. The kitty is thankful, expressing appreciation. He calls out names, and from the broken front door behind us skitter out three small to medium-sized dogs. An orange cat stays in the doorway watching. I think they're supposed to show gratitude. I can't remember their names.

Mona sings, "Little dogs, little dogs, wherefore art thou? Orange kitty, white kitty, where thou art for? What's going on, Ya? Little doggies! Little kitties!"

I sing, "Auspicious as fuck!"

"Dogs and cats living together — "

She's all smiles, then the animals begin to withdraw. She caterwauls, "No, don't go! We're animal people!"

"You're a Megatherium!"

"Hello there!" hollers a voice, that has us whip it!

Whipping around…but we already know who it is. Two doods. It's the fed and the so called civilian. Out of uniform? They have flashlights. At least, the civilian looking guy has a pink cowboy shirt on. It's faded, and it's under a couple layers I can tell. The fed doesn't show any pink. The lights skim over us. We squint.

Mona dives to her pack with her vodka, pulls out two plastic masks, a clown and a witch. She gives me the witch. We put on our masks.

Mona does a commanding voice: "Nothing to see here!" She goes drone: "Move on, move on."

The two men stride up the broken path to the steps as only doods can stride, with confidence and calm and threat. The dogs and cats have disappeared.

The civilian calls, "Wild night in Saginaw. Bonfire you could see from space." He turns off his flashlight, gives it a shake. "It's dying down."

The cropped suit fed goes, "What if we're from the future? And we've come back to see our origin from this rough time. What would you say to the future?"

Mona flings, "*From* this rough time? Or *in* this rough time? See what I mean? Coming or going? Pitcher or catcher? Listen up, Mr. Man, cats and dogs living together. We got the word from an old tom who lives 'round here. Goes by Cat A. Lyst. That's Lyst with a Y."

The fed is open-mouthed, bewitched by her essence! He fumbles, "You are too smart for your own good. B-T-W, your photos didn't come out."

He's shining his light in Mona's clown eyes. I sing, "Hey, hey, go away! Get that light off her clown!"

He aims the light down. Good boy! Big boy behavior.

I say, "You guys got it all wrong. We're a clown, a witch, on the biggest night of the year. Yes, strays at the moment. But this moment's broken away from history, so from fluency."

Mona queries, "How do you mean?" Her clown tilts its head all funny. Inquisitive!

"Well, broken away from making sense. So ready to go any way. The denouement can go any witch way. Doesn't have to be bestial at all. Only humans act this way."

The fed snarks, "Armed and partying. That's the 21st Century."

Mona says, "You're not listening. Dogs and cats living together? Hear what she's saying! This moment is armed and partied to flux!"

The civilian shakes his head, pulling at his face, rubbing his mouth, twisting his ears. "Hey, I always loved witches. Like at Halloween. But clowns are spooky. Don't ask me. Some folks just feel that way. You guys, we're not here to hassle you. We wanted to make sure — "

Mona blurts, "Don't filibuster my flux!"

The fed interrupts: "The Painter. We need the Painter."

Mona says, "I know! You guys should wear these masks back to the party and do your *Spy vs Spy* thing."

I say, "The kitty said there's a rumble tonight. The Naco Curs are gonna hit the Saginaw Runaways."

"Wow," goes Mona. "I did not know that."

Her happy face, clown face, plastic color cover! She is so on! I'm *inside* my own plastic cover. Worrying my essence...perky...coltish...wearing a mask is peeking out. Witchy.

I gurgle, "'Change was in the air'. That's what you tell those future folks." I reach over to touch Mona's hair, push it back behind her ear.

The civilian, who seems humaner, goes, "Look, you guys, something's going on, the pink, the shootout. Don't get yourselves mixed up in something."

So not too human.

There's a horrendous crash followed immediately by screams. Mona and I are on our feet, packs fixed, masks pulled away.

The civilian snaps on his flashlight.

The fed whelps, "What was that?"

The civilian says, "Come on." He turns and trots away. The fed follows.

Mona says, "I'm afraid to look."

"We owe it to the Runaways. Let's go."

It's quick up the path to the road then over a bit, to full frontal, face-to-face calamity. The porch collapsed. People are running every which way, streaming from the house, then jumping down past the mess of porch and people splintered together. People tear out of the front yard, zigging to their cars and trucks, zagging up the road on foot. Cars and trucks ignite to power. Luckily, the bonfire has died down. Embers cast a weepy glare on the chaos. No one seems to be on fire. The music is off. Imploring voices, pleading cries make their own wall of decibels. Random screams — ghastly. We don't know what to do, how we can help, but we know we have to try. We dodge our way in to the melee.

People guide the fallen out of the porch ruins. It's a mass of mess of sticks and boards. Flashlights are focused. Stoners and drunks do their best to help. There's the civilian and the fed in the middle of it. The bad boys are nowhere to be seen. I can tell because most of these folks wear pink. We head over by the civilian. He glances up and nods. He's getting a guy up from the mess on the ground. The guy seems okay.

The civilian says, "We were lucky. No one seems to be injured, just banged up a bit. The fire died down or the whole place would've gone up. Everyone was so stoned and drunk, they sorta bounced when the porch collapsed."

Mona says, "Not much of a drop, thank the goddess."

We offer a hand to people untangling from debris. Check for blood, breaks. Hold their hands, nod and smile. Screams settle down. Now it's the honking that blares, cars and trucks marking their skedaddle, porch collapse sound track, everybody scrambling for cover. There's still a lot of people making sure everybody's okay. Some managed to stay on their feet, so walked away. Others fell on top of each other. The ones who happened to be on the bottom are the ones we're worried about. We're helping as we can, poking through wreckage. Men wrestle with the kegs, gotta get them down from the doorway, now no steps. Mona calls me to where she's helping. I cut across boards, through red cups, bottles, a muddy pink scarf.

Mona says, "Check it out."

Where the porch attached to the house is now exposed. The foundation wall, that the porch was up against, that holds up the house, is right there in front of us. This concrete wall shows a word, in big pink letters, spray painted across it: "PAINT!"

Painter must have crawled under the porch.

He must have done it before. "Right?" I say aloud.

Mona shrugs, looks uncertain. Her eyebrows are up!

He must have done it before the porch collapsed, but he wouldn't have known the porch was going to collapse. He had to get out in time. Or else he would be smashed like a bug.

Mona points to the flooring piled before the pink word. "We should check." She spazzes like a tiger.

We pick our way through boards and junk. Does seem to pile up here.

A bulge, a rise, a bump —

"Oh, no!" I cry, and Mona and I tear away boards fast as we can.

Beanpole dood. Will is under the rubble. He seems to be breathing. No bones sticking out. Or guts sprayed about. His layers protected him. He's covered in filth.

Hands and face scratched and bleeding. We kneel by him but are afraid to touch him because his spine could be snapped. I decide it's okay to brush away splinters and dirt from his face.

Mona calls, "Need some help over here!"

Will sputters, "No, no, no." He turns his head to puke. He spits, settles, breathes more evenly. We help him to a sitting position. He says, "I'm fine. My family's got no money for doctors. I'm on probation. I gotta get out of here." He pushes at us, feebly moving us back, then he tries to get to his feet. He slurps back to the rubble, gasping.

"Hang on, hang on," says Mona. "You're in shock. We're all in shock. You'll get away in time. You know how parole officers are anywho."

He stares at Mona: "People see it?"

She nods.

He looks at me: "Donna okay?"

I nod hopefully.

People see the boy. They see the pink word. Not necessarily connected. People get it. Stand and look. No one knows what to do. People point, fake laugh, wave away.

We're in shock and it's a good shock, as we realize how much worse it could have been. Like we're in a story that changes course, then changes again and again, spiraling as the party pinks out even more.

We get Will to his feet. No questions asked. Mona leads him away. I take his other side.

My little Nightingale. I really like her hair like that.

Who knew the porch would collapse? This crowd, our crowd, our town, and we knew the porch was going to collapse. We're used to that kind of thing. Our biggest night of the year. Cats and dogs living together. The stars blotted out. This is a lousy moment, so the perfect moment. No other moment available.

Will says he's fine, spazzes away from us, goes to look for Donna.

I turn up, tune in, tell off: "To Old Town! Let's get this Budinski thing going!"

People start yelling, chanting, "Old Town!" And: "Paint the town!" Lots of "Pink! Pink! Pink!" shouted over and over.

New scramble to leave! The long line of vehicles has been making its way out of Saginaw for a while. It can't go on forever.

Mona's beside me. She teases, "Let's get a ride," and winks.

Cecil shows up, walking right in to me. I say, "Hey, Cecil. You're bleeding, man. Your forehead?"

"No time," he mutters. "Looking for my dood — you seen him?"

"Who you looking for?"

He's either stoned out of his head, or in shock, or undergoing the transformation. It's all in the timing. He could be a zombie crammed full of smelt. He swims away, goes in search —

Men and woman float around, bobbing, taking the noise and air and vibes, bending with them, stirring, pretending there's a direction. *Get outta here!* Really, they did help, they were helpers. *Gotta get a ride!*

Mona and I, out on the road. More horns, and lotta yelling and yakety yak. Small groups. Begs for rides. At least it's not raining. Damp air can only dampen. Will they head for Old Town? Finish this thing? A moving mess of a party. What time is it? I don't think it's midnight. But it's gotta be close.

Mona says, "If you see a pickup with room in the back, jump on."

"Mona," I say, "I need to tell you about it."

Mona lips, "For reals," a little squeals —

Vehicles crawl along. Actually, we're walking faster than they're driving. We slow down. Mona turns to me. Eyeballs to eycballs, we do our fizzy exchange.

She sings, "'By the pricking of my thumbs — '"

A pickup comes up behind us. It interrupts her melody. Now we're all eyes for its room in the back. We yell to the driver if it's okay. He nods and hoots, the people up front with him hoot, the people in back chime in. We climb aboard. A girl and two boys in back. We're all smiles and hoots, and it's cold and wet, but our smiles could circumnavigate the globe.

Mona and I cuddle in the corner, against the tailgate. We make it to the highway, and things go fast. Horns are more intermittent, and echo-y. It's a long, stretched out line of lit up vehicles for the last few miles to Old Town. We curl around the pit, but can't see in to its entrance to hell.

Mona says close to my ear, "Deets!"

I go into it: "Once upon a time, a girl was running in a crack in the Earth, and far ahead on the trail she saw a flat, white stone with this word on it: AYADEMAVICHY."

Mona squeals, "Vichy!"

"The crack was clogged and the girl wished for a giant paw to clear her way down the trail. A giant ground sloth appeared and cleared the way, then the beast, now her friend and ally, was attacked by conquistadors. I saw this."

The girl across from us has blue lips, but she manages to say, "You guys are tripping."

"I know," I say. "Vichy."

"Visions of 'vichy', my dear dead girl. Pink girl! You're on fire. Your Asperger's syndrome has taken a loop de loop through your notochord."

"Silly. But that's when it happened. I saw the men dump the pink. That very day, in the arroyo."

"Who — what?"

"Ted and Hector. I saw the whole thing."

"You *did* know it was there. I knew it. The pink, I mean." Mona pulls around her pack, goes in search, pulls out the vodka. She wiggles the bottle at me. I take a hit. She has one. We pass it around.

The girl with blue lips takes a hit, says, "I can't feel

any more."

Mona says, "Right now, cause you're freezing your ass off? Or do you mean, in general, in the cosmic sense?"

Blue Lips says, "What's a girl to do at the end of the world? Can I sit by you? Cuddle me!"

Mona says "We're almost there, sweetie."

I scoot over to her. Mona sighs, comes along. We slide to either side of the girl. Push in. She cuddles.

We get off at the exit to Coltrane. Right into Old Town. Smallville on acid. Pleasantville. Pretendville. *Death don't have no mercy!* Cars and trucks honking up the place, as they barrel around to park. People fill the streets. Maybe people heard all the commotion and came out to see what was going on. People can feel these kinds of things. The more, the merrier! When our ride slows to a stop sign, Mona and I are poised to leap, the others as well. We climb out, glance around for Blue Lips. She's disappeared, swallowed up — .

Right away, we spot painters with spray cans taking care of walls, steps, fences, signs. Pink! Pink everywhere. The tags are simple, 'pink' in pink, 'painter' in pink. We run up to a guy with a spray can who's finishing his 'painter' tag. He tosses the spray can to Mona and runs off. That's the way it is: zoom over, blammo! Do it, get out fast. Take cover, amoebas!

Mona takes the can, zips along the street, dodging and dipping through people and vibes. I'm with her, beside her, behind her. We feel it together. Laser beams tripping the light fantastic! The galaxy cracks open like a can of beans! Mona's covered in halos — geysers. She's trying to be indiscreet/discrete. Might as well tell the sun to hide. She steers clear to her spot, a fresh, unpainted wall. Actually, it's a culvert, but who care? She has to jump down. I stay up top lookouting. She flames on, pink sizzling like a hissing snake from the can, a pink, aerosol rope of serpent. She writes '*azul* across the bareness in pink.

"Get it," says Mona, appraising her work. She shakes the can. "Almost out."

"You're messing with their heads."

"Civilians."

That's when the sirens start.

Mona forces the spray can into a crack in a wall. "Stay!" she commands, flashing her open palms to secure the spell. I help her up. We merge with the crowd.

Sirens — out of tune but breaking our eardrums. All sorts of law enforcement vehicles, lights whirling, hustle in to town. Red lights add perfect glow drop cherries to top off the party. Law enforcement parks, turns off the sirens. A bigger vehicle has followed the cruisers in. This is a black metal dump truck monster. The big truck stops making sense, sure enough it opens in the back. Doods all decked out, cyber-ninjas tromp tromp tromping out. Oh, I see, they think this is civil war. They line up, keeping their riot guns down. The law enforcement guys from the flashing cruisers saunter over to the ninjas for a chat. Robots peeps' blinks. The crowd does an awful bony, phlegmy hurrah! Thumbs up! Blazing scorch like they've turned cannibal and need meat. The sheriff and police chief take a stroll. They're coming. The sheriff's got a bullhorn.

The crowd has turned into margarine, a cheap

nebula, a fiercely spiraling, living entropy of failures and reprobates. They're screeched up, sphincters hot, ready to charge or vacate, at a moment's notice. Talking, laughing, yelling, hooting, come back full power. Mona takes my hand. So much fun, so much threat, so much pink, so many looks required.

The crowd expects pus and nematocysts. That's the truck they load the werewolves in.

Somehow, we're in front of the crowd. Mass of humans behind us giving the snake eye to the ninjas, deputies, police, whoever else stands opposed.

The sheriff holds the megaphone to his mouth, talks, "This is an unlawful assembly. Vandalism is a serious crime."

I climb up a car, step up to its top top, face the crowd. I yell, "The evening is young! We're not done! Party!"

The response is alarming, as it's an answer in a tremendous roar: "Party!"

Mona is ten feet tall. I can see her. Everybody could be on stilts. Everything can expand. Everyone can expose.

I keep skitching, "Only one thing left to do tonight, and that's to go to where it started. It's almost midnight! You want to know where the pink came from? Where it all got started? The Painter will be revealed!"

The people are positively jubilant, screeching back, "Pink! Pink! Pink!"

I finish with, "To Greenbrush Draw! We'll meet out there off Naco Highway and see where the pink got started. Let's go meet the Painter!"

Tear gas canisters plop in and say hello.

Chapter Twelve

TED::

"How come she didn't like me? The kids liked me. I could tell. I can tell when a person doesn't like me. Read it plain as a book in front of my face."

Hector doesn't even twitch. Petrified dood. Rock lord. He's leaning back. He looks baked. But it's late. Extra dark. We've been out for hours on the dirt roads again, because we had to clear out of Cecilia's earlier than expected. We'd been laying low, waiting for our call, counting orbs and ovals. I napped. I can't see him hardly across from me. He said he couldn't sleep. Maybe he's two thirds asleep. Maybe half.

I found a half a box of rice crispy squares behind my seat. Out dated a year, so as we say: *only a year, have no fear!*

It's before midnight, New Year's Eve, and we're hurtling down the highway one more time. This is it: the big delivery. Old Town's in such a uproar we don't have to worry about tails. No one out at all. Everyone's in Coltrane whooping it up. We. Can. Do. This.

Who could have known that woman was going to be so sensitive? I affect people that way. They either like me, or really dislike me. Should I say this to Hector? He's too out of it. Practically living in the truck these past couple days, with the surprise in back. Surprise, surprise. Women don't like husky guys unless they got money. Yeah, sure, she was a good looking MILF, and she got all Final Jeopardy on my ass before I had a chance. Maybe she didn't like me because I'm a big fat slob of a loser. Maybe she didn't like me because I got a truck, connections. I got it going on. The kids ended up liking me.

Hector grrrs like a dog but I can make out: "What time is it?"

I burp and fart, roll down the window.

"You're alive!" I roll up the window.

He's getting his shit together, pulling himself upright, pushing his shoulders back, scanning out the window the whole time. He says, "We're almost there."

"Home again, Flanigan! Didn't think we'd be back so quick. But no one will be looking out here."

"You got those pink animal stories."

"Nobody cares about that. Easy peasy — "

"Stop. This has *got* to go smooth. Not like last time. We deliver it. We don't even touch it. In and out like the wind."

"Like the wind."

I go on, "While you were daydreaming, I figured what it was."

He doesn't say anything, or even look my way. I think if I poked him, he'd snap around and bite my hand off.

I say, "D-E. Encryption Device. Ultimate, universal D-E. The key that opens any lock."

"Wouldn't that be E-D? Or, maybe, a *decryption* device. D-D? All we know is its worth human lives."

"So, a weapon!"

"Don't. Why speculate? Dump it. We're outta here!""

"I don't see how we can screw this up. It's gonna go smooth like you say. I brought extra underwear." I fake laugh, but it is true. I did bring extra underwear.

Hector gasps out an actual half-assed laugh. I got him going!

"What's your favorite book? I want to know. On account of you told that girl, Kaylen, but you never told me."

"Did you read *Lord of the Rings?*"

I laugh and slap my thigh. "Shit, man, I read *The Hobbit.* Loved it. Some of the first one, 'Friendship of the Ring'."

"We're about there."

"So tell me. Why not?"

"In case I get wacked?"

"Very funny."

"*Vandenberg* by Oliver Lange."

"Is that real? Is there such a thing?"

"What did Dollar say?"

"I already told you."

"*Uno mas, por favor.*"

"Mr. Dollar said, midnight wherever I wanted. I told him here. Greenbrush Draw. He's the only one who knows. We're getting there early. Beat the rush. Mr. Dollar takes control of the item, we are out of there. Course he gives us something extra for our trouble. He owes us! Then, see, the way this works, now he can sell it to the highest bidder, whatever the heck it is. Obviously, people are interested. And we get a cut of that, too. Extra extra. That's what he said, he promised, he won't forget us, that's what he said."

Hector sighs out an okay.

"You're worrying. I can tell. That woman made you all touchy feely. Right? Questioning shit?"

"What the fuck — " he says.

I glance over at him with a big doofus grin. He smiles back through the dark, letting up a bit. He says, "You're a goof, man."

MARCO::

"Shoot out at the OK Corral!"

Yankees and their commitment to violence. Force! It's been two days since the shootout at the dollar store, but Eddy still can't calm down. The saga of the West, civilizing and conquering the savage, when all along, no one could figure who was the savage and who was the civilized. "Now what? Why am I here?"

I'm involved whether I want to be or not. I don't have a gun. I don't carry a gun in my car. I carry binoculars. I have a shotgun and a hunting rifle at the house. I can tell by Eddy's stern, thin lipped look that he's got a plan.

"Marco, they used us. We have such a sweet operation going, we got soft, and these *pendejos* took advantage. They used us, our connections, our truck. They figured we're soft, so they'd get away with it. But, see, the truck took off before they nabbed it. No one's got the goods. It's up for grabs. It's not over, Marco. We're not done."

"We got paid."

New Year's Eve I should be in the backyard, star gazing with *mi familia*. But Eddy's my guy. He won't sit, insists on standing there, before my desk, as though asserting his annoyance. "We've been over this a hundred ways." I depend on him. I trust him. I want him to know that. "What's up? What do we do?"

He nods, glad that's over. "We got a reputation to hold up. Marco, it ain't about the money. Course that's important. But, see, the cargo's out there, right now, teasing us, in play, anyone can get it."

"You want to get it first, so we get our reputation back. Prove we're solid. Man — "

Now he looks tough and mean, like you wouldn't want to be around him in a bar fight: "Our guarantee is everything. That's our name." He's disgusted he has to say this. "I know people on both sides. I hear things. In Arizona, last week, people talking about pink animals. Conejos. Pink rabbits. The gente are getting nuttier than usual over there. Good cover. We slip over, get it, slip back."

I know where this cartoon is going. Shouldn't I have my hired goons take care of this? I don't have any hired goons! Whether I like it or not — I go, "That load of barrels that went through a few days ago? Pink stuff. Same guys as two nights ago?"

Eddy nods. "Same guys. Our guys. Ted — it's his truck. He's...reliable, but a dumb ass. When the shooting started, they took off with the load. Smart! When I talked to the guy from the dollar store, he was digging, trying to see if I heard anything. He didn't know where those guys were. Must be worth a lot more money than we figured. I mean, whole lot of dinero."

"He didn't think it strange you calling him?"

"I said I was worried about our truckers. He cut me off, afraid they were listening in."

"What is it?"

"Who cares? It's a load. It's a dollar."

I grumble, "They either got rid of the load by now or stashed it. What? They still have it and are driving around? That would be stupid. I bet anything they sold it.

It's been a couple days. I don't get it. Pick up, delivery. We set it up. That's our job. Why would these guys mess up their own delivery?"

Eddy thinks it's obvious. "Jefe! They pay us to set it up. We're known, no one notices us. It's a sure thing. The truckers pick it up, dollar store guy pays the truckers on delivery. Then they pay dollar store guy for that delivery. They're cutting out the middle man."

I shake my head. I try not to yawn. I need a coffee. Some Hornitos. "Then why set it up this way? Dollar store guy must be pissed. Yeah. Still, it doesn't make sense. People out there, looking now. The cargo, whatever it is, it must be *muy* valuable. After the shoot-em-up, the truckers gotta be running scared. Homeland Security. Way too risky."

Eddy knows where I'm going with this so jumps in: "Pendejos! I bet anything they're hiding, waiting to hear from the dollar store guy. They sure ain't gonna talk to the hombres with the guns. Andale! One of my guys — he calls from Coltrane, and he says the Americans are rioting. Fuck! Who knows? But he thought it had something to do with the pink shit. They're fighting cops, man. They called out the army. Ha! He said, they're all supposed to drive to Greenbrush Draw to meet up. Just up the road from here." He shakes his head, uses his chin and lips to point north. He's itchy for it. "Something's happening. We check it out."

"Why there?" I recall birding there. This arroyo. Quail. Towhees. Thrashers.

Eddy says, "Suppose Ted couldn't sell the pink? Follow me?"

"Yeah?"

"Pink animals in Naco, see what I mean? Put it together. Easy place to dump it."

"The pink got dumped?" I sigh. I broil. I am not. I am. "Then, why in the world would they go back there?"

"That's why I called you. It's loco, don't make no sense, so you know that's what the gringos are doing. My boys are out, driving around, keeping their eyes open."

"But what does this have to do with the thing in the truck?" He lets me work it out. "They won't go back there — no way. Unless they figure — suppose they figure it's the last place anybody would expect? So, so, so, a good place to get rid of it, for the final delivery. And they have no idea what they're walking into. It's fantastic! We have no proof. Nada."

"We have to get it before Señor Dinero. We get it, we hold an auction." He nodded, grunted, smiled.

"If we get it first. How?"

"Something's going down. We're on it. Watching, waiting. The truck's too obvious. They ain't coming here. Greenbrush Draw? At the arroyo? Who knows? Got eyes on it. We'll know pretty quick. But you're right, maybe nothing."

"I don't get it. Why are all these people going out there tonight?"

"They're dumb shits. Rosa has bewitched them. That's why we gotta be ready, before the truckers get killed and lose the load. That's why we're here. That's why I got you here tonight."

LUCUS::

I can't believe we're heading out to Greenbrush Draw, going on midnight. But tonight's partner in crime, my fibby, tells me it's our duty to keep our eyes open. *She* said to head out here and he heard it, and that's where we're going. Is she leading the way? This is where the arrow points. It's way too pre-ordained, like a set up. How seriously is he taking this pink dealio? Whenever things get so...fated, I want to run the other way. No way, inevitable. No options. Well, keep moving. That's what we're doing now. This time, though, the goofy off duty adventure doesn't seem ironic. It seems out right. A weakness in the story line gone non-linear. We're supposed to follow? I guess it's because of those two girls. Because they're obviously involved. I say, "What's with the girls?"

It's his car. Not nearly as scratched up as I assumed it would be. Not bad at all, comfortable, new, smells fresh, like him. He glances at me. "We're almost there. All systems on. They're spraying now."

I look confused I guess, so he says, "I got feeds, data coming in. Back up."

I assume that's what he means.

No one in our office seemed too interested in Greenbrush Draw. What happened in Saginaw and Coltrane is a blip in the history of drunks at the end of the world. Even though they did call out the troops. Question is, what have my partner's people cooked up? My conviction about the connection between pink and shootout is now more of a shrug of a coincidence. But what's driving him? His conviction they're related? What was in the back of the truck? Follow the Painter, get the truck, discover the shooters. This is a lot bigger than I imagine? He's got to be fixed on the cargo. It's gotta be something! Damn! He's searching, planning, dreaming of the precious cargo, following every lead. I'd say that's what's behind this.

Of course, he's driving, and, apparently, he did actually hear the one girl tell the crowd to head here, where the pink began. Sorry, I missed that. I was stopping a fist fight between two hefty biker women. A few cars and trucks ahead of us, behind us. She has legions! The Painter's going back to the source.

I guess tonight's partner — the way he looks means he's been thinking it over. He's concerned. Not good. In a fire fight, you go with your gut about what's best for the guy next to you. That's automatic, not something you think over.

Finally, he says, "Maybe you meet a person with incredible energy flaring out in geysers a couple times in a lifetime. Anybody can see it, feel it. Deputy, do you see auras? Whether you are aware of it or not, there's a lot of science backing this up. People trying to figure out what human energy is. What are vibes? Chi?" He wavers, comes back. "I figure someone could get hurt." Now he shrugs, mutters something I can't make out, and I don't ask him to repeat it. Then: "Maybe once or twice in a lifetime...you meet a person...they ...mesmerize?"

"Those little Naco girls? Dood, you're in love."

WILL::

Cars and a truck follow us to the culvert, by where Mya lives. Tonight, people will follow anybody. We park. Doors open. People laughing, talking. Pink peeps join us.

Everybody's looking around. Who will lead us, they be thinking. We rally. We function.

I cry, "Short cut! No worries! We know the way to the pink! We went for a run here a couple days ago. It's not far. I swear! We got flashlights. We can do this!"

I didn't break anything — it's adrenaline. That's all. The rushing comes from what happened in Saginaw, but I made it. I did it. I got away.

"Okay," I call, "follow me to the pink! Where it all got started. Down here, then straight up the middle! There's a good trail right down the middle. There's a path. We got flashlights. It's too cold for rattlesnakes. Not too cold for us. Let's go."

OTIS::

For some reason, give Will and Donna a ride, then I'm following him, like the dick is a leader, into the draw. What a doof! But it's easy and we hit the trail like a bunch of bozos. No sweat. What a bunch of wimps and losers. Who are these people? I've never seen these people before in my life. Will and that little Donna — would not be pretty to watch. These others: Dork-o-ramas. Disgusting, out of shape. How'd I end up with the weirdoes? Old people! Hippies! I should never have left my boys tonight, back in town. This. This could be good. Fuck it! The way Mya said it, all tense and sharp up on top of that car roof — she was like a goddess. Where is she? She must be at the pink already.

DONNA::

My pink face feels ceramic. I'm becoming a teapot. My head feels with steeping. We're going back to the arroyo where we run. Will speaks up. Otis is wobbly. Will gets in front. He's in charge. Back to the pink. Otis is grumpy. The other kids giggle. Old couples. Hippies. I count them. Twelve peeps. Walking down the middle. I think they are mainly altered. Will's altered. It was he who suggested our experiment — him / me. He says it will release endorphins in our brains. Both of us. That boy.

QUENTIN::

This girl is so lush, her skin pops firecrackers everywhere it's exposed, where I see it, where I touch it. I've never had such a buzzthrill with a girl, who tells me where to put my tongue. Tongue goes everywhere on her. She is so ripe, but she has no clue if she doesn't want to do it, too many beers, not tonight. Basically, means we ain't going there. I have a clue but I'm not. There's a moment a guy enters when he's had a boner so long, it pokes the very continuum, distorting time/space to an ache from hell. She wanted to come so much, to do what Mya said about coming out to the draw. Donna said she knew a shortcut. Now we're behind Donna, walking down the middle of a crack in the Earth, with boners blazing. Do girls get boners? Here we are, ready to pink out.

SEÑOR DINERO::

Set my lurps out early. Clear a path. Take a reading. Go in crispy. Set up a perimeter.

Delivery. Pick up the goods. Ted and Hector. I know them. Good boys. They'll be expecting payment. Fine. Give 'em something.

So many looking for them. Should have — they have no clue. Running on empty. Which may be to their advantage. Retards are unnoticeable. Vehicles at night, these days, are noticeable.

Sure, Greenbrush Draw, good as any place. I'm on my way.

Trying to stiff us! It's all set up nice and pretty, and he thought he could interdict delivery! I'm going to put a bullet right between that terrorist's eyes. We pick up the load. I get the word out. Auction.

Trying to mess with me — we had an agreement, a done deal!

The sixty-four billion dollar question is why the damn terrorists set the deal up this way. They wanted an easy, safe border crossing without questions. For sure. They went to Eddy who went to the truckers. So why put me in the deal as delivery guy — then try to shoot me? They didn't have the second half of the payment that would go to me and the truckers? Set up of the set up! New players — somebody trying to cut in?

Don't overthink it. One step at a time. We pick it up. Boom!

The way that guy was, when he tried to take over. His *compadres* looked scared. But him? I'm thinking ramped up vet. Ex-marine going on a bender. The others had no control of him. That man is dangerous. Has to be put down. He'll be the one to target. I am going to kill him good. If I ever see that guy again —

What the hell! What's going on? All this traffic?

PHILIP::

"Look, Troy, the others want me to talk to you."

"Out here, brother? In the bushes? You brought me out here to give me the good news, the low down, the what for?"

"Troy, someone could have been killed."

"If I'd wanted to kill anybody, I would have."

"That's what I was afraid of. Hell of a lot of bullets — look at our truck!"

Troy meanders over to the little white truck, pats its hood. He sighs, not remembering all the holes. "It's a decent truck," he says. "First thing you learn in a firefight is people's aim goes to shit."

"You were counting on that."

He pffts. "Go ahead. Lay it on me."

"We've all been out, looking for the big truck. We been watching the back roads. The safe house, the new car, are only good for a while. We give it one more day."

"We're running. Get ready to bolt! That's what you brought me out here to say?"

"Huh? We've been compromised."

"And if I don't go quietly, you leave me in the bushes."

"Oh, stop it. People know the truckers."

"I told you it was a dumb set up. Wasting our funds. We could have got it across. I could have done it."

"Gotcha. I don't want to go over it again. Twenty-four hours."

"Of course it's my fault. I went all rogue on your ass and blew it up. There's only one thing to do now and that's for me to commit hari-kari with my butcher knife inoculated in the toxic hell of Iran."

"We could've been killed."

"We find the truck, we get our goods. Boom! We're out of here! No sweat! My spidey senses are thrumming. It's going down!"

"It's too hot." I'm breathing hard.

"Soon!"

"Troy."

"Philip, Philip." He does the exaggerated shaking of the head. In my flashlight light, it looks ominous. "My little brother with the cause up his ass. Are you noticing anything besides your despair? Not sure why you brought me out here to Naco Highway. I mean, if you're not gonna whack me. But check it out. Look at the traffic, Philip. What's going on? Where's everybody going? Maybe we should go see. Just for funzies."

"We'll be spotted."

"It's ours. Okay? We're still in play. This isn't over. Besides, now I got 'em scared of me. You said you wanted my help. All of you agreed. I said fine. I said I'm security. There was an opening, I took it. Misjudgment on my part. We go on. Try again."

"Troy, this isn't war. Not yet, anyway. I'm not sure. But secrecy is essential, or the entire operation falls apart. We can't call attention to any part of the...riff."

"The 'riff'? I know what isotopes are. Why pay that extra dood? See how that works?"

"The isotopes are worth — "

"You said! That's why we have to get them back. How does it go, Fearless Leader, about what this riff is to accomplish? No? You won't say. You think I'm making fun. Okay — I'll say it: you guys sneak this shit in to the big seed factories, and it makes like a radioactive tracer on GM food, its DNA. Everybody knows about DNA now. Then consumers get their little toy Geiger counters from their breakfast cereal boxes. Consumers will never be misled again to think they're eating real food, when, instead, in fact, they're eating Frankenfood. Power to the people! I done pretty good?"

"It's nuclear material, Troy. That's all Homeland Security will see. We have to stop the madness. In a collapse, the first thing to go is the food supply. People have to know what they're eating. The operation is jeopardized. Twenty-four hours. Going down in a blaze of glory can't be the answer."

"Let's see where everybody's going."

MONA::

Cecil can drive. "Cecil, can you drive?" I say from the back seat. At first, I went to sit up front in Adam Waserly's car (whom we call Atom Wazoo), but Cecil, who's driving, said he wanted Mya up front. I'm in the back with a passed out Atom. If he pukes on Mya's pink jacket: pink retribution! Pink salvation!

Cecil still hasn't answered, but he's proceeding along carefully, like a Driver's Ed teacher, out of town, heading for the highway that'll swing us around towards Naco, back to the arroyo.

Too many cars. Are they following us? Are we leading? Do they know the Queen of Pink New Year is with us? Not at this pace.

She emits pink pheromones now. Maybe that's what made her a friend to the giant ground sloth. Pink made flesh and flash. Pink in our rush, pink in the pink death of slippery pink night.

I say, "I think everyone's following everyone else. Maybe we can get in front. You know where to turn off, Mya?"

"Brilliant," she says. Then: "Cecil, your head? You okay?"

"I'm fine."

Mya asks, "Is this the dood you were looking for?"

"Yeah. This guy found the dump on scorpions. He knows stuff. Gotta watch out for him."

"Good for you," she says.

Our drive out of town leads gossamer —

Hello, night!

Later, that night —

I say, "Mya, what's going to happen when we get to Greenbrush Draw?"

Mya says, "We should take Naco Highway, then I'll say when to turn off. What do you think, Cecil?"

He grunts, hits the turn down Naco highway, mumbling something about his mom or how they live on the same street.

I try again: "Blind leading the blind, one eyed leading the one eyed. Last time, we went the other way. I walked, you ran in. Peeps be wandering for days out here, on the dirt roads, in the stickers and sloths, lost, lost, peeing their pants, running out of water and food, resorting to cannibalism."

Mya says, "Maze of dirt trails. Did I tell you how delicious you look tonight?"

I strain to hear but that's it. Cecil drives very carefully. Cars near us offer up prayerful honks. Pink supplication! What time is it? This moment's bubble is building and building —

Then Mya goes, "When we see pinky, where it started, we will remember what should be here and what should not. This is not a dump, no matter how blast zone."

Cecil mutters now like a Wookie on acid: "Dump! Dump — it's a dump. A dump! The mothership! Earthship! Blast zone, dump. Blast zone, dump." He starts nodding. The nodding goes ballistic. Great big old nods that writhe his whole upper torso. The car swerves. He slows, lets a car go around, pushes restart —

LUCUS::

The first rule of a fire fight is know where everyone is. Second, keep moving, don't let the bad guys know where you are. Impossible here. Well, sure, I can see where everyone is, but sitting in the car, windows down, staring out in disbelief, I know there's no way I'm gonna be able to keep a position. Way too many civilians. What did they spray? WTF!

It's like a desert night revival, or like a drive-in movie of a summer evening, all lit up in headlights and flashlights. Swarm in progress, and damn if that's not Koontz's truck with another truck, a regular size green pickup, backed up to its rear. It could be green. Rear to rear. It's going down! Back up.

We're warming up the cactus and converting the mesquite. We make an arc of vehicles in the brush. Impossible to figure this, how it will go down. A half moon of cars and trucks, headlights shining zebra swaths of light stabs. The arc centers around the mating trucks. Trucks! Where's the little white one?

Vehicles keep coming, honking, whooping, emptying their loads. Shouts from the draw! "Pink! Pink!" Sounds like kids. Kids must have come up the draw like before. People gather in twos and threes, walking around, making it over to the draw, passing the big truck, flashlights on the pink. An old guy, standing by the rear to rear trucks with a few other men, starts yelling. I suddenly recognize him from the dollar store.

"Keep back! Keep away! What the hell you folks doing here? Got a private transaction going on here. Keep away! None of your business."

Meanwhile, voices: "What's going on?"

"Who are these people?"

"Where's the pink?"

"Painter!"

"Happy new year!"

"There's the pink!"

"Down there!"

"Look! See!"

"Freaking me out! No way!"

"Let's get outta here."

"Could be toxic!"

The people are waking to something isn't quite right. Kids climb out of the draw. The guys around the trucks look dangerous. Koontz. He steps away from the men, goes with one guy, to the truck's cab. No hightailing it out of here tonight.

"Where's that girl?" inhales my buddy, my partner in crime.

"What a mess!" I cry.

A tall, skinny boy, who came from the draw, hollers by the big truck: "This is it! The place! This is where the pink started. Come see the pink. Bring your flashlights."

He's too close to the truck and the old man jumps around yelling, "Get outta here!"

Headlights go off, go on. People at the edge, looking down, pointing and talking.

Koontz and his buddy come back from the cab, moving around to the back of the truck. Koontz messes with a lock, hefts the lever, the back of the truck sweeps up.

"We played this well," says my partner.

"What's gonna happen?"

He studies his vehicle's rearview mirror. At first I think he's mesmerized with his own dull brown eyes, but something's got his attention, something of interest. He says, "That little white truck."

We get out of his car. We check our weapons. I am flushed in it. In a few seconds —

I repeat, "Back up?"

"Occupado. Armed... suspects, civilians. Far too many. Layers upon layers of backup, goods, bads, I'm afraid."

"Whose people?"

"*Fata morgana.*"

"You're tripping?"

"You'll see."

The little white truck barrels in, swings around, scattering folks, and backs to the mating trucks. The doods by the big truck watch, watch, then all at once that watching festers a rage, the old man jabbering away at his guys. Had no clue Koontz was so hardcore. The occupants of the small truck are two white men. The driver gets out. The old man steps forward. Other men, in and out of shadows, from the crowd, from the bushes, surface, hover around. What the hell! Cops? Bodyguards? *Sicarios?* How many guys the dollar store have? Scanning this light show, hombres materialize like tumors. Goods? Bads? How to tell? All this dust — barely see...night dust. The driver of the little white truck climbs up on the hood.

He yells, "Don't know what you people are doing here. We got business here. We'll get our stuff and go. But we'd appreciate it, if you stayed back. We don't want no trouble."

The old man spits back with, "Oh, you've got trouble, asshole. You got a whole lot of trouble coming your way. You go for your gun and you are dead. You have ten seconds to get down from there and get back in your truck and get the hell out of here."

I see the two girls, walking in with a young man. No way. Too many guns. Too many wackos. Too many triggers. It's the old crossing of the streams of chance routine. The braid that goes one place.

"Now," says my partner.

MONA::

Mya and I, finally, calm Cecil enough, so we get out of the car, all three of us, leave Atom asleep in the back. Mya had Cecil park close to the highway. For a quick getaway, she said. All these people. So many showed up. For pink? For Mya? Ha! For yet another desert blast zone bash! Where's the keg? What's that big truck doing there?

This guy climbs on top of this little white truck and starts yelling.

Mya bends in close to me to say, "I'm bleeding."

Yes, you are, my pink ground sloth, my pink desert queen, my pink painter lady!

I say, "I owe you a band aid."

All at once, a flicker, a sparkle in the air. Like when a certain slant of light, whether night light or sun light, coaxes vision to suddenly the air is crowded as a science fair aquarium. Not just dust, particulate matter. Lifeforms undreamt of. One of those eye flutters blinks a second — re-focus. Arrange floaters in *Nude Descending a Staircase.* Major movie mirage. Ah! Something's in the air. Something can't be blue balls of phosphorescence over our busy parking lot. Headlights. Glow sticks are green. Prism play. People are luminous orbs. Ploys. Looks like the cover of an old science fiction magazine. Maybe a special f/x eye candy dream — where are the crystal towers and cubes of steel? In the future, everyone will be pink. No non sequiturs. The lives demand it. This future. Holograms. Got to be. Vision occluded. Can't see Mya beside me.

This flaming goddess of pure pink lava power stands alongside me.

We've stopped. Stagger. But the vibe's pliant. I would guess everybody's digging it. Maybe not. Fulfilling bad, bad fulfills, and fills —

Cecil cries, "Mya — " and bends over to puke.

Mya goes, "No big."

Flicker snaps back. Parking lot of the future meets Mad Max Jetson's.

What is real? What is *our* real?

SEÑOR DINERO::

Who are all these people? Got to be feds! Fibbies are here! Bring it on! Their fancy antsy bullshit. Rain of terror? Prompts. Preclusions. Goes to show, people are so dumb they're smart. They don't dare interfere! Not with the crowd. My guys? Here. Perfect. That's where they are. I am going to kill that guy and nobody can stop me.

MARCO::

Cars and pickups parked along the highway on both sides. Looks like some big to do. In America, either a lynching or a church service. Eddy manages to park so we can get away fast. We're partially hidden. Whatever. Commotion, yelling, honking, people! It doesn't make sense, but we're here, we're going to check it out. We walk in. Eddy says his boys are here. What the hell. We come in slow and easy. The big truck. I see it first in the play of lights. Eddy spots it. Eddy's geared tight and seeing that truck, he's got the strangest half smile I've ever seen on him. How did he know? Then Eddy recognizes another truck. He says that's the little white truck from the shooting match.

People. Vehicles. Bird brains. I'm tripping. It's insane!

Everybody knows. Everyone's after the load.

How could they know?

I gotta get out of here. Fuck. Eddy's got a pistol.

TROY::

Shooters to the left of me, shooters to the right of me. *O, sphere of influence!* I don't even sneer at their Cointelpro. Dumb shits — gives them the shakes. Drones — must be. Look at these civilians, look at the sheep led to slaughter. Not a clue. I don't even stumble atop the little white truck. Hesitation? Is confusion. Eat it up! I practically live on it. Delicious chaos! Release. I eat it up. Then, me bro, panic in his eyes, leans out of the truck to eyeball me, going, "Come on! Let's go! Now!"

No.

TED::

Hector scoots around, going back and forth, like a sentry. Contrails. WTF! Fireballs. Faces! Faces made of rubber, or they look like plastic figures, like my collectible peeps grown up. So Hector looks like a faery-Ninja-warrior. It stabilizes. I can breathe. I can swallow. Fucking A! Well, mainly, I read auras, but these are envelopes. Cages mages mazes. I step forward and yell out, "No funny bidness! Or we dump it in the draw! I will! You know I will!"

MONA::

The peeps will claw off their faces and eat their lips on tortillas. Pure chaos tastes like sin that gives in. Like there's nothing else but sin surrender. Screeching prepares. Cecil stumbles when he tries to walk. Mya goes to him. I hear her whisper, "Go back to the car, wait for us. Take care of Atom."

Mya sees that look, says those guys with the big truck are the ones that dumped the pink. Crunchy, crackly, crazy shouts: "I'm tripping! "Tripping!"

Now the fat guy from the big truck says they're gonna push 'it' in the draw. Mya belts out a 'no' like she's not kidding around. She takes off. More pink? How much pink can we take?

LUCUS::

Mya shoots by — what's she saying? 'No'?

My battle buddy's way too unctuous. But no way this little reality check's gonna slow this avalanche. They're already tripping most of the time. No way any of this could fit an algorithm working the battlefield.

Surprise, surprise. He's got LSD eyes. Now what's he gonna do —

He buzzes off. Zig zag. Jerky. Mechanical. Then stops and stands, straight up and proud. He moves on slowly. Don't draw your weapon, you fool! He doesn't. But I can see the way his hand snakes over. I'm to the side of him, ready to hit the dirt, when he's close enough to announce to the circle of firepower: "This is the FBI. Drop your weapons immediately! The area is surrounded. I want everyone to line up right now, make a line here in front of these trucks. Right now!"

That's just great.

Screams!

People run for it. They bump in to each other. People fall down. People walk into thorns. Vehicles rev up. The circle stands secure. No one has dropped a weapon. Fiesta of the lit. Flashlight dance. Cars and trucks scramble away.

When out of the brush, an arc of official goons, in full battle regalia, stalks forth.

The guy on the little white truck pulls a gun.

Koontz at the big truck screeches, "Hector!"

Bullets fly.

DONNA::

Will throws himself over me, knocking me down, him on top of me. He does this when the popping and smoke begin. Like firecrackers. Oh, Will, you're altered!

QUENTIN::

"Right now, with you in the draw with me, I love the smell of napalm in the evening."

"Quentin, I like you and everything, but you're a bit of a dick. What are they doing up there? What's going on? What's that noise? We should get up there and see!"

MYA::

I scream, "Stop! Stop! Stop!"

EDDY::

Death don't have no mercy in this land!

Americans set it up so there's always a lot of easy kills. What I mean is they act like they're asking for it. They're so stupid about proving toughness, but they don't know enough about hate to pull it off. Real hate comes from a lifetime of scrambling to survive. Americans don't hate good. They've watched too much TV about good guys or about doing the right thing. That dissipates hate. They pretend. But we're all Americans now. And revenge is always just.

LUCUS::

My boy charges with gun blazing. He's targeting the guy on the white truck, then the guys shooting at the guy on the white truck, all the while screaming, "Hold your fire! Hold your fire! Ceasefire!"

Crossfire! I laugh, I cry. I'm already flat on my stomach, in the dust, weapon out. I scuttle for some brush. Guy on truck's down. Screams! I don't know a way out. Shooting stops. Cav to the rescue! Shouts of "Drop your weapon!" "Get down!" "Get down! On the ground, now!"

My boy's down —

SEÑOR DINERO::

Ramon's down. My best boy. Twenty years! But I got him, I nailed that terrorist. Got him good. I know I did. I kneel down by Ramon, as it stops. Suddenly, cops everywhere! I know I have to go, but Ramon —

PHILIP::

When the shooting stops, I drag Troy into the back of the pickup, on account of the bullets knocked him to the ground. He's got holes through him. I'll drive.

Uh-ho.

Who are those guys?

MYA::

"Look what you've done!"

I cry. "Help them!"

HECTOR::

I put down my fists and get down on the ground beside him, and I lean over him on my knees to look at his face, see if he's breathing. I unclench my fists. The shooting's stopped.

He's mumbling, sputtering. I make out: "Gut shot. Don't worry, I'm insulated. Tell them, when they're in there, to turn on the lipo. Maybe that lady will like me then."

ASTRA::

This screaming girl's covered in blood with a guy on top of her. So much blood. I've never seen anything like it.

Suddenly, I hate my flashlight.

So much blood. I'm gonna vomit! I have to help.

What happened? What's going on?

Should I hide? Run, run! Hide!

The shooting stopped.

I keep my flashlight on them. The boy fell on top of her. He's the one shot. Did he jump on top of her to shield her? The girl's losing it. I bend in, grab her wet hand. The flashlight makes blood deep scarlet, shadowed blood is black. She can't get up. I release her hand and pull back on the boy's shoulder. Light as a feather. Tall, spindly dood. He's gone. I kind of roll him to the side. I get her up, wrap my arms around her, and let her scream.

"It's over," I say. "It's over. Are you okay? I don't think you're hit? I think you're okay. Your friend protected you. My name's Astra. I'm from Coltrane. Help is on its way."

Now she weeps.

I say, "Let's walk over here."

Cars and trucks every which way. People running. Like army guys? Bodies. Folks try to help, kneeling by the bodies.

It seems over.

O God.

Engines blast. Exhaust clouds mix with dust clouds.

The girl can't stop, and the copious tears clean the blood from her pink face.

People on the ground in pools of what looks like oil. Are the pools steaming?

Gunpowder air.

I will not scream —

Lucus::

I leave my battle buddy dead on the sand. I go over to Mya who's standing like I guess she's in shock. I don't see any holes in her.

I say, "Mya, Mona's hit. Help is on its way. Ambulances on their way."

She tears around, stomps by me, back the way I came, to Mona.

Mona. Blood gurgling out of her mouth.

Mya says, "Look at her lips."

"Mya, she's bad."

Mya leans in to kiss her. When she comes up, she's got blood all over her face and front, and Mona's stopped gurgling.

ASTRA::

The girl's name is Donna, and when she realizes we're walking away from her boy, she squeals and pulls back. I hold her, coax her. Tell her we're not going anywhere. Just over here. In the open area by the big truck. Some people are there. It's okay, I go.

Then, I think: should we run? Hide until help arrives?

Is that a helicopter?

Just in case the lunatics with guns start up again. But help has arrived. I think.

This young woman stands right in the center. The weird lighting has her painted black, down her mouth and chin. She's got a bloody front, blood all over her face. She begins loud, and, soon as Donna hears her voice, she stops struggling.

"You men have screwed things up — all of history. It doesn't work! Why don't you learn? The killing's got to stop!"

The words come out in a cackle. Wrenched from the precipice. I turn Donna towards her.

The young woman sees Donna. They move to each other, falling into each other's arms.

Donna sobs, "I'm bleeding. Mya, I'm bleeding."

Mya says, "Me, too. The Earth weeps for lost life."

Mya turns away from us, her arms shoot straight up, hands out, fingers spread. She yells: "The killing's got to stop! This way is death. Only death. We choose life."

Voices cry out. Soldiers tromp in.

Donna wails.

Tears pour down my face.

Donna and Mya know what to do. First, they thrust their hands in to their pants, then pull them out wet with menstrual blood. And then they move to bodies, prone on the ground, dead bodies with holes in them. And they kneel by the dead and touch their faces. Then they touch their bloody fingerprints to the faces of all the men standing around the dead. The men pull away! They panic. They don't know what to do. But they can't resist the girls' touch. The army wants to intervene, to stop the girls.

Donna whips around. "No!" she cries. "Don't you dare!"

They do the men by the big truck. This little white truck. Two other bodies farther back.

Oh, what are we doing?

Too sad!

Right — necessary to touch the blood.

Everyone's so afraid of blood.

Oh, what are we doing?

Blood of death. Blood of life.

This horrific moment —

Men shrink, jerk away. Shouts of 'no!' "Get away!"

Too late. Too much!

All the women there start anointing the men.

It's easy for women to replenish our blood supply.

We paint the faces of death with life blood and seal this horror with life.

Born in 1951 in the Ozarks, Chris Dietz is a writer, teacher, and a birdwatcher. Currently, he lives in Bisbee, Arizona, surviving a catastrophe.